*Other books by T.J. Mindancer . . .*

# HEKOLATIS'
# PROMISE

# HEKOLATIS' PROMISE

## T.J. MINDANCER

TALES OF EMORIA

Bink Books
Bedazzled Ink Publishing Company • Fairfield, California

978-1-945805-28-8 paperback

Cover art
by

*A Mindancer Book*

Bedazzled Ink Publishing, LLC
Fairfield, California
http://www.bedazzledink.com/

*For all the faithful fans
of the Emoria tales.*

This story takes place in the world created for the original
*Tales of Emoria: The Saga of Jame and Tigh.*

# Chapter 1

TREE.

Heko glanced back through the chaos of bramble and trees and glaring streaks of sunlight. She grabbed the lowest branch of the squat mountain oak and hurled herself onto it.

She focused her senses on the path she had just followed. The aroma of moist earth filtered through rotted leaves tickled her nostrils. Even a mountain cat with steps like feathers couldn't hide nature's perfume, and her trackers were mere humans.

Not fifty paces away, three warriors moved like shadows through the dapple of sunlight in dense spring leaves as they scrutinized the upper branches of the trees.

*Idiot. Of course they'll check the trees.*

She slid around the trunk, careful of the treacherous knots and haggard bark, away from the eyes of her hunters.

*Now what do I do? If I only had something to . . .*

She mentally slapped her forehead. Now she understood why old Wencer made them carry a handful of small stones. The oldest warriors' trick. *Which means . . .*

She fished a few stones out of her pouch and, with as much noise as a mouse whisper, tossed them close to the sliver of water off a ferny incline near the hunters.

The warriors stopped and twisted around, looking like fantastical gaila birds from the blinding sun-sparks dancing off their armor. Bracers blazed as hand signals joined the warriors' indecision and, after several tense heartbeats, they disappeared into the ferns.

*Which means the old trick still works.*

Heko dropped out of the tree and crouched in the undergrowth. She opened her senses to her trackers. They were far down the creek. She ghosted through a new growth of aspen and past a lichen-encrusted statue of Laur holding a waterfall in her cupped hands.

She got to the high mountain creek, chuckling with runoff from the spring snowmelt, and knew she had lost time eluding her hunters. *Balance*, Wencer's voice shouted in her mind. Decisions were always made with balanced thoughts, or a warrior could find herself between a sword and a boulder.

On the other side of the blade, a part of balanced thinking was to know when to take chances. If her hunters thought she was across the ferny tributary, then she could win back her lost time and then some by taking the elk trail just around the jumble of boulders downstream.

Her body kicked into a jog before her mind told her to run. *The body has its own instinct. Learn to pay attention to it.*

For the first time in three days, Heko felt as if she wasn't walking on glass shards and reveled in the crunch of fine rock as she ran along the creek bank. She sucked in the mountain air—barely touched by the warmth that blanketed the lower valleys that time of year. Snow was possible in Emoria, even that late in spring, but enough warmth remained after the frigid winter to feel wonderful as the air pricked the exposed skin between the patchwork of leather and armor.

She rounded one of the many boulders that sprouted from the forest like dragons' teeth—at least they looked like dragons' teeth according to ancient tales. The trail became little more than a series of flattened-grass footfalls through a splotch of meadow, green with young grass and pastel with the first wildflowers of spring. A half-grown elk foraged the young shoots.

"So elks really do use the elk trail." Heko doubled her pace. She dismissed the fleeting thought of going around the beast and laughed as she dived over it. She rolled to her feet and sprinted into a stand of trees.

She laughed and startled nesting birds and unseen critters among the leaves. She couldn't help it. After three days with only brief naps and the food she had foraged from plants, she was beyond caring if her trackers heard her or not. Her exhaustion and hunger nourished rather than depleted her strength as she entered the old growth forest.

The sun broke through the still frozen mists. The day was only halfway to midday. A real meal and afterward her own bed to sleep in. Soon. She focused on old Keilie's lamb stew and thick-crust bread as the trail rose and dipped and twisted through a steep hill of boulders.

Sure-footed as a mountain goat, she didn't disturb as much as a loose stone as she leapt and jogged up and over the hill into a shallow valley of new-growth trees. She loved the stories about how her people spent a summer, after fire swept across the valley, clearing the burnt trees to allow the sun to touch the seedlings already taking hold.

Heko jumped from the elk trail onto the dirt road. She ran down the hard-packed middle to avoid the deep ruts that had to wait for the ground to thaw before groups of young Emorans poured out of the city on repair patrol.

She tapped into a reservoir of energy and sprinted the last stretch of road.

The three trackers stepped onto the road a short fifty paces in front of her. Too close for her to slow her pace and think of a way to avoid them—not with them running toward her.

"Laur's waterfalls. How did they get here so fast?" she muttered.

She spotted a thin overhanging branch and pushed off with her toes. Sending frantic prayers to Laur, she grasped the branch and brought her legs up out of the reach of her hunters. Their frustrated shouts touched her ears as she swung her body forward and released the branch. She kicked her long body into a ball and landed in a roll. Within a heartbeat she was on her feet and thirty paces away. Her shoulder hurt like it had been whopped by the broad side of a sword. The half-frozen dirt was as hard a rock.

Thank Laur her hunters were just as exhausted as she was, even if they had eaten better during the three days of the hunt. Their sluggish response surprised her a bit. They were seasoned warriors and trackers, perhaps only ten or fifteen years her senior—in their prime and well-respected in Emoria. Yet she didn't hear them behind her.

Heko plunged into the cave at the base of the white rock cliff that was the last barrier of defense into Emor canyon. She ran so fast she risked extinguishing the torches in the wall sconces maintained by the outer guards. Almost there. Almost there, and her hunters weren't behind her.

She bolted into the canyon of Emor and cast away her caution. She didn't even have to think. Just run the length of the deep canyon of white rock. The light dusting of snow on the new grass surprised her. But Emor canyon did tend to have its own weather, and its isolation seemed to hold the cold long into spring.

She sprinted past the masked outer guards who stood vigil in the meadow and pulled her strength out of the air as she closed in on the wall pocked with irregular-shaped openings. The larger holes were fronted by bulges of rock, and she could see pairs of masked heads visible over the lips of these bulges.

The road curved to the wall, close to where the gate stood open for her. The pockets protruding from the adjacent cliff wall also had watching masked faces. Heko mentally shook her head. Emorans had to find their entertainment when they could—even in a common initiation ritual.

Heko dashed through the shallow tunnel into the city of Emor. She glanced up at the white cliffs. Curious faces peeked out of doorways and windows all the way up the walls. Down on the square proper, women loitered in the doorways of shops and residences and gathered in knots of casual curiosity.

Heko slowed her pace, her footfalls echoing in the expectant stillness, and stopped in front of the three women gathered next to the central fountain. With relief, she noted her breathing was not too labored, and she was only a little light-headed. Too many initiates had collapsed and even fainted when they had reached the end of their test. Before they had a chance to hear the words of their queen.

She put her hands behind her back. "I return with all the half-braids."

Wencer stepped forward, bent her gray head, and counted the braids on Heko's belt. "All the braids are accounted for." She returned to her place.

Hyek, Queen of Emoria, stepped forward. Her blonde hair had a few gray streaks, but she was as strong and competent as any warrior in her prime. She gazed into Heko's exhausted eyes. "You've brought honor to our house and you've brought honor to Emoria this day. Your performance gives us hope that the next generation of warriors will continue to be the best in the Federation."

Heko bowed her head. "Thank you, my queen. My life is dedicated to protecting the honor of our house and of Emoria."

A smile touched Hyek's lips. "You've always set a good example for your generation. You've made this heart proud today."

Heko stared at her mother. "I . . . I . . ." Her knees buckled, She stared dumbfounded at the hands that grabbed her as she slumped to the ground.


HEKO OPENED HER eyes and blinked up at the polished stone of her chamber's ceiling. She shook the fuzziness from her brain. She felt like she'd been asleep for a half-moon. The familiar comfort of her chamber was strangely alien after three days outdoors with only a small blanket and her knowledge of the land to keep her safe and warm. Alien because the chamber was exactly the way it had been before her initiation, down to the fire chattering in the fireplace on the far wall. The ordinariness of her cavern chamber with sunlight filtering through thick opaque glass on the cliff-side almost diminished the immense change she felt within herself. She'd changed, and she wasn't sure if she could face her everyday life as if the change hadn't happened.

She pushed up on her elbows and turned toward the aroma of food. A pair of lidded pots sat on the small warming shelf in front of the fire. It must have been about the time they expected her to wake up because old Keilie never let food warm for too long.

The aroma permeated the part of her brain that went straight to her stomach. She had fallen asleep before she had a chance to fill her belly.

She stretched with care. Her calf muscles were a little sore, and her shoulder had a bit of a tweak in it but not bad at the end of an exhausting three days of being hunted.

"About time you woke up."

Heko jumped. "Laur's waterfalls, Taine."

She sat up. Someone had stripped off her weapons, grimy leathers, and boots and got her into her sleep shirt. Her body was still covered with dirt, and she wrinkled her nose. Food first, and then a long soak.

She eased out of the bed, ran her hand through her shaggy hair, and grimaced at how filthy it felt.

A head covered with shaggy dark curls popped around the leather and twig chair that faced the fire. "You're looking especially becoming this morning."

"Glad to be a part of your daily entertainment." Heko padded to the fireplace, pulled a pair of fire pads off a hook, and picked up the containers by their metal handles. She then carried them to the small table and sat down.

Taine grinned as she joined Heko at the table. "You're always a part of my daily entertainment."

Heko shook her head as she scooped out morning dumplings and egg in milk gravy onto a plate someone from the kitchens had remembered to leave for her. They had warned her that first meals after initiation were always bland. As much as her imagination had run to mounds of goat stew and thick slices of brown bread when she had been out in the forest, she had to admit the dumplings were about all her stomach could handle. She lifted the lid off the second container and released the heavenly aroma of the spiced tea that was like life's blood for Emorans.

"Wencer said for you to eat slowly." Taine nodded at the plate.

Heko stuck her fork into a dumpling and resisted the impulse to devour the plateful in three bites.

"You really surprised them, you know." Taine poured spiced tea into a mug and slid it to Heko.

Heko swallowed a mouthful and gave Taine a puzzled look. "Surprised them?"

"They never actually saw you until right outside the tunnel." Taine poured tea into the guest mug she had liberated from the hearth and took a sip.

Heko piled dumplings and egg onto the fork. "That was the idea."

"That was the idea but no one ever does it—at least not until the second or third day," Taine said.

Heko frowned and pondered Taine's words as she chewed. "Not being seen was the easy part."

Taine put down her mug and stared at Heko. "You had Jyger, Ques, and Pyam on your trail."

Heko pointed the empty fork at Taine. "They were looking for me, not trailing me."

"What's the difference?" Taine asked.

"The difference is between knowing and not knowing where I am," Heko said. "They were trying to find me, not following my trail."

Taine gave her a knowing look. "And how did that happen?"

"They trailed me as far as the waterfall in Laur's canyon. I slipped into the cavern behind the falls."

Taine frowned. "I can't believe they didn't check the cavern."

Heko nodded into her mug and took a sip of the mind-soothing tea. "Ques braved the cold water and searched the cavern."

"It's so shallow. How did she miss you?"

"A fortnight ago I anchored a rope in the little cave halfway up the falls. I entered the lower cavern, climbed the rope to the little cave, and pulled the rope up. The falls are so heavy this time of year, I had to be careful to avoid the pounding water, but it hid the rocks above the main cave."

"So they guessed which way you went and left the falls and then what?" Taine put her chin on her hand.

Heko shrugged. "I followed them for two days and two nights."

Taine straightened. "That's even more amazing than them not seeing you. You successfully tracked them without them knowing it." She snapped her fingers. "That's how you retrieved the half braids. You took them after they abandoned waiting for you at each place."

Heko popped the last bite of food into her mouth. "I just kept out of earshot behind them. On the third day I turned around to head back, as they did, and that was the only time they almost caught me near the river. But I used the old throwing the stones trick to get away."

Taine shook with laughter. "They're not going to be happy to know that really was you. They thought it was a deer."

"Thank that deer, then, for allowing me time to get away in the opposite direction. They must have given up after that and set the ambush in the outer meadow since they knew I had to cross it."

"Where you jumped right over them."

Heko sipped her tea. "I was surprised they didn't catch me. Any one of them could have flipped after me, half asleep."

Taine gave her an incredulous look. "You're kidding. Right? They said you were so quick you were almost to the tunnel by the time they turned around. And the tunnel sentries said the same thing."

Heko shrugged and drained her tea. "I think they were just exhausted."

"Believe what you want," Taine said. "But don't be surprised at the stories that will come of it."

# Chapter 2

TAINE STOPPED IN the opened doorway of Heko's chamber. Heko had certainly grown and matured since the last time she had put on her best leathers and armor and combed her hair so it looked almost manageable.

She had to admit the negligent tousled look and the well-worn everyday leathers were endearingly appealing on Heko. That look complemented her impish blue eyes and cute face. It also fit her natural bashfulness from being the reluctant center of attention since birth. She thought it ironic that Heko's attempts to look and act like everyone else had the reverse effect because she wore the persona so well.

Taine was not immune to Heko's charms, and caught herself when she realized she was staring. She had outgrown her crush on Heko, and treasured their solid friendship. They'd do anything for each other only for the asking but they weren't destined to become life companions. They shared what Emorans called blood love—a bond as strong as a family's.

Taine sauntered into the chamber. "I'm glad you don't walk around looking like that all the time."

Heko stopped adjusting the leather braid laced with purple strips of cloth that hung from her belt and gave Taine a blank look.

Taine grinned. "Everyone would be running into walls and smacking themselves with their own swords."

Heko scowled and returned her attention to the braid. "I'm no Cesle."

Taine shrugged. "Cesle is only interested in other women looking at her. And she's interested in more—if she can get it. Hyek says there's someone like Cesle in every generation. Someone who tempts our virtue and fidelity."

"The temptation wasn't that great if they were anything like Cesle." Heko straightened and made sure the patchwork of leather and extra armor fell into place. She picked up her polished sword, slipped it into the scabbard on her back, and put her two ceremonial daggers through the side lacing on her boots. "I feel like an idiot."

Taine walked around Heko, pretending to evaluate her. "Idiot is not the word I would choose."

"If I didn't have to go through with this to get my braid, I wouldn't." Heko shook out her shoulders to settle the extra armor.

"You look great. No matter what you think," Taine said. "I know several scouts who wouldn't mind being seen in your company."

"You scouts are only interested in warriors because you don't have what it takes to be one." Heko ducked Taine's playful swipe.

"You warriors like scouts because you can avoid all the gashes and broken bones during courtship." Taine adjusted the leather braid around Heko's forehead and centered the small medallion with a crossed sword and bow that hung from the braid on short strands of silver.

"Warriors courting each other should never use swords while sparring." Heko's expression was solemn. "Their feelings blind their judgment."

"Something you've never experienced firsthand." Taine stepped back and nodded at her handiwork.

"Thank Laur," Heko said.

Taine shook a finger. "Ah, your time will come."

Heko straightened her armored bracers. "You won't find me mooning over someone like you mooned over Reisen last season."

Taine put her hands on her hips. "I didn't moon over her."

"You took her to the festival of flowers," Heko said.

Taine shrugged but the memory made her smile. "That was fun but I think we just didn't have enough in common."

"You've always been more open to the idea of finding someone." Heko walked to the fireplace and covered the fire with ash.

"You've been more focused on finding yourself first."

Heko looked over her shoulder. "Don't let old Faev hear you. She'll make you apprentice in the Archives."

Taine wrinkled her nose. "Ugh. Don't even think such thoughts."

Heko laughed as she walked to the door. "Come on. Before Hyek sends the guards to get me."


HEKO WALKED THE last few steps up the path and stopped on the edge of the south rim of the city, gazed across the meadow, and was not surprised to see most of the population of Emor gathered around the low stone ceremonial circle. She couldn't even participate in something as common as a braid ceremony without a fuss.

She looked down the path carved into the walls of the city below them. Taine had stopped just beneath ground level to rake her hands through her hair. "Trying to catch someone's eye?"

Taine scowled and lowered her hands. "Habit."

"You'd better watch it or some impressionable acolyte is going to think you need to be joined to her," Heko said.

Taine straightened. "Acolyte? You wound me, warrior." She climbed the path and stood next to Heko. "Whoa. The whole city's up here."

Heko sighed and trudged on the crushed rock path to between the stone pillars of Trigo into the ceremonial circle of low, flat stones. White flowers had replaced the snow that had dusted the meadow on her last day in the warriors' camp before her initiation. That had been only seven days ago, but it felt like another life.

She walked across the circle and stopped in front of the platform on the far edge. She glanced back to see Taine join the crowd gathered just outside the circle of stones. She faced forward, where her mothers waited with Wencer on the platform. She knew Hyek had to a keep a solemn demeanor but her birth mother Niko's expression shouted her pride.

Wencer, full-armored and as formidable as when she commanded the forces in the Phytian Wars, strode off the platform and stood a pace away from Heko. She crossed her arms and made a show of inspecting her princess.

"It seems Laur thinks this youngster is woman enough to take her place among the ranks of the greatest warriors in the world." She raised her eyes to the spectators. "She has bested the best hunters and trackers in Emoria but that was just a child's game compared to what she has to face before the warrior's braid is hers." She clasped her hands behind her back and sauntered up to Heko. "Are you ready to meet this final challenge, Hekolatis Ketlas, princess of Emoria?"

Heko set her jaw and braced herself. "Yes, Master Warrior."

Wencer grinned, stepped forward, and planted a kiss on Heko's lips. "The traditional kiss of mentor to pupil has been executed."

Heko knew that the warmth in her cheeks was a blush. Why did the older women enjoy embarrassing the younger warriors? They had a hard enough time being teased by the other warriors when a young woman showed the slightest hint of romantic interest.

The crowd whooped and laughed. The fact that every warrior had to endure this humiliation helped, but Heko wished that she hadn't reacted with a blush. The warriors wouldn't tease her about the kiss, but a blush was ample kindle for their endless jibes.

Hyek descended the three steps of the platform. Wencer stepped back several paces so Hyek could take her place in front of Heko. Their eyes met, and Heko forgot about her embarrassment and her red cheeks as she witnessed the pride and love in her mother's eyes.

Hyek held up a braid laced with green-dyed leather. "A queen has the honor of presenting many warrior braids, but to have that honor as a mother is about the greatest gift Laur can give, other than the actual gift of the daughter." She smiled at Heko. "Hekolatis Ketlas, princess of Emoria, I present you with the braid worn by warriors of Emoria from before our recorded history." She tied the braid to Heko's belt and looked up and held Heko's eyes for several heartbeats as if to memorize the moment. She then returned to the platform.

Wencer unsheathed her sword. "Hekolatis."

Heko straightened. "Yes, Master Warrior."

"Pledge your sword to your queen and to Emoria."

Heko slipped her gleaming sword from its scabbard. With her sword in her hand, she felt a control that had been missing since she walked onto the meadow. She was a warrior and was comfortable only when she was being a warrior. She extended her arm and sword toward Hyek. "I pledge my sword and my life, to defend Emoria and the citizens of Emoria, to never dishonor my sword with personal revenge, to always honor and respect my queen and my country." She whipped the sword into a salute.

The meadow erupted in cheers, startling the spring birds off their nests.

Heko finally relaxed and allowed a rare smile.


HEKO HEARD CRUNCHING footfalls coming her way but she didn't turn from gazing at the mountain peaks on the western border of Emoria. How many times through the years had she stood on that spot while her imagination spun harrowing adventures beyond that wall of stone and snow?

The women who had witnessed the ceremony had descended back into Emor. The sounds of Heko's comrades rose up from the barracks on the eastern edge of the meadow as they prepared for a day of sparring and training.

"I know that look," Taine said.

"What look would that be?" Heko turned to Taine.

"That look you get when you're thinking about going exploring."

"I'm thinking of going to Balderon," Heko said. "Niko's sister runs the blades shop there."

Taine frowned. "What would you do in a city? I thought for sure you would go to little Emor to practice warrioring in the swamps."

Heko sighed. "I know my mothers are worried about what I plan to do out there. I can at least give them the peace of mind by staying close in Balderon, doing nothing more dangerous than learning the art of making and selling knives and swords."

Taine kicked at a stump of grass. "It'll be strange around here without you."

Heko cocked her head and nudged Taine with her shoulder. "Why don't you come with me? You have your braid. You're free to choose what you want to do now."

Taine stared at Heko. "Come along?"

"It'll be fun." Heko snapped out of her pensive mood. It *would* be fun.

Taine wrinkled her nose. "Learning the sword and knife trade?"

"Learning about life by exploring Balderon and spending evenings in the safe house," Heko said.

"Ah, the safe house." Taine's eyes sparkled with a wicked glint. "Women from all over the territories. I thought you weren't interested in matters of the heart."

"I'm interested in their lives," Heko said. "What life is like out there."

"I heard they're more interested in what it's like to cozy up to an Emoran." Taine straightened and took a couple of swaggering steps and turned around. "Visiting Balderon might be fun."

Heko grinned. "You just want to flirt with some of those delicate merchant women. I know the type you're attracted to."

"Just because Reisen was in training as an acolyte . . ."

"The delicate type makes Laur's decision easier when choosing a birth mother," Heko said.

Taine's eyes widened. "I'm not ready to be thinking about a life mate."

"You're just ready to think about having some fun before one of those girls following you around decides to trap you." Heko laughed at Taine's indignant expression. "They seem to like your roguish charm."

"You're the one with the roguish charm." Taine put her hands on her hips. "If I happen to want to discover the wonders of the women outside of Emoria, I think you just want to get away from all the attention here."

Heko studied the distant mountain peaks. "I can't get away from thinking they're just interested because of who I am. I want to be someplace where no one knows who I am, and who will treat me like everyone else."

# Chapter 3

HEKO MANEUVERED HER horse around an outcropping of stone and pulled back on the reins. Her horse danced on the loose stones of the trail before settling down. She stared in wide-eyed awe at the endless grasses bounded by hazy hills. The wall of the city of Balderon was a thin line on the far side of the valley.

"Laur's waterfalls." Taine pulled back on her rein and her horse clattered to a stop beside Heko's. "That's Balderon?" Her voice twisted with uncertainty.

"It's much larger than Rihnon," Heko said.

"And I thought Rihnon was huge," Taine said. "How many people live there?"

Heko gave her an amused look. "More than in Rihnon."

Taine sucked in a nervous breath. "Do you think it's hard living in a city like that?"

"The safe house and blades shop are in the middle of the city." Heko shaded her eyes against the intense overhead sun. "Our sisters seem to be able to live, surrounded by all those people."

Taine nodded, still looking a bit uncertain. "I guess this wouldn't be much of an adventure if it were the same as living in Emoria. We can certainly do anything our sisters can. More."

Heko grinned and, with Taine following, guided her horse down the tight switchbacks of the trail into the valley. They trotted onto the spring grass, and for the first time on their journey, Heko felt carefree.

"Race you to the gate," she shouted.

They kicked their horses into a gallop, and the long grass flowed around them like the waters of a mountain lake.

Heko felt as if she had been curled in a tight ball all her life and finally could stretch out to her full height. The sun's warmth awakened all of her springtime longings and a lifetime of wishes for adventure.

She yodeled battle cries, echoed by an exuberant Taine.

The rough stone walls of Balderon grew from a thin line on the horizon to a barrier of huge blocks of fitted rock that loomed above them as they trotted to the eastern gate. A man stepped out of the small gatehouse to the side of the opened archway.

Heko stared, and Taine's eyes widened in astonishment.

The gatekeeper rubbed his beard as he studied them. "The blades shop is straight ahead. On the left side of the central square."

Heko's jaw dropped at the sound of his voice. She glanced at Taine, who looked like she'd been smacked in the head.

Heko realized they looked like idiots. "Straight ahead. Thank you."

Heko kicked Taine with her stirruped foot. Taine blinked at her and gave her head a shake. Heko nudged her horse. Taine pushed her horse after her, and they trotted through the gate.

Heko pulled her horse to a halt. Taine stopped, her eyes so wide, Heko thought she was going to turn around and bolt through the gate into the open grasslands.

People in bright exotic clothing, horses, wagons, carriages, buildings of stone and wood crammed together. Noise. Too much noise. But more than that . . .

"That was . . . those are . . ."

"Men." Heko gave Taine a quick look. "Don't stare."

Taine turned to Heko. "Me? Your jaw is dragging on the ground."

Heko straightened and snapped her jaw shut. "I never imagined them just walking around all over the place."

Taine tried not to wrinkle her nose. "They're awful hairy."

"We'd better get to the safe house." Heko nudged her horse past a trio of women in tailored tunics bordered with delicately stitched design. The women looked them over with unconcealed interest. She glanced back at Taine, who stared dumbfounded at the women. "Taine."

The women giggled as Taine pushed her horse next to Heko's. "Did you see how forward those women were? What a strange place this is. Men all over the place, and women showing blatant interest in public with everyone watching."

"Jyger told me what we see as bold and forward is just being friendly," Heko said.

"That's just being friendly?" Taine's voice cracked. "I'd hate to see them when they're really interested."

"Come on." Heko kicked her horse forward. "Our sisters will explain everything to us."

Heko tried to focus on the road as they pushed past too many people and horses and too much noise and strange smells and . . . men

. . . men . . . everywhere. Strange hairy creatures with human bodies and human features.

The road spilled into a round plaza that could easily hold the whole city of Emor.

"Laur's waterfalls," Taine rasped.

Heko studied the buildings that bordered the plaza. "There it is."

Taine let out a long breath of relief. "Thank Laur."

They guided their horses to the east side of the plaza and dismounted in front of the blue-painted door with a crossed bow and sword on it. Heko was glad to see Taine's hands shaking as much as her insides quaked. How did her countrywomen live in such a place?

"Where do we stable our horses?" Taine asked.

Heko looked around. The buildings of different heights were jammed up against each other except where a lane or road broke away from the vast cobblestone plaza.

Heko handed her reins to Taine. "I'll find out." She went to the blue door and knocked. A small panel slid open, then closed. The door opened, and a woman with graying hair and strong features gave Heko an admiring look.

"What do we do with our horses?" Heko asked.

"Lise," the woman barked over her shoulder. "I'm Pakl, proprietor."

"I'm Heko. That's Taine."

Lise rushed past Pakl and skidded to a stop and stared wide-eyed at Heko. Heko took the reins of both horses from Taine and held them out to her. Lise continued to stare dumbfounded.

Heko looked at Taine, who was trying not to laugh. She finally put the reins in Lise's hands, and Lise looked as if she was about to perish from a massive attack of hero worship. Wearing a silly smile, she led the horses away.

"I think you'll blend right in. No problem." Taine maintained an innocent expression at Heko's scowl.

Pakl led them down the narrow corridor to the common room, which was half-filled with mostly young Emorans. "The bunk rooms are full right now but we have a two bed room on the second floor."

"That'll be fine." Heko looked around the chamber. Weapons hung on the walls over murals of Emoran heroes. The tables and benches were rough-hewed wood with sturdy Emoran bronze plates and tankards scattered in front of the Emorans, who seemed to have stopped in mid-action to stare at her.

"Nara can use a couple more hands if you're planning to learn the blades trade," Pakl said.

"That's why we're here." Heko frowned at the staring women. She glanced back at Taine. "Do I have mud splattered on my face or something?"

Taine laughed and pushed a confounded Heko after Pakl who led them up the steps on the back wall.

"LAUR'S WATERFALLS," TALER squeaked. "Who was that? She looked like she just walked out of a fireside tale."

"Do you think she trained her hair to fall onto her forehead like that?" Ange cuddled her tankard of ale between her hands. "And those eyes. I could stare into eyes like that all day."

"I could stare at all of her all day," Taler said.

"I wonder if that scout with her is her sweetheart." Ange took a sip of ale.

"Someone like that has dozens of sweethearts," Taler said.

Ange raised an eyebrow. "So you think she broke all the hearts in Emoria and is expanding her territory of conquest?"

"I wouldn't mind losing that battle." Taler sighed as she put her chin on her folded hands.

"You know that's never going to happen," Ange said. "I've yet to see a homeland warrior show any interest in romantic pursuit."

Lise ran into the common room from the kitchen corridor. She skidded up to Taler and Ange's table and plopped down onto the bench. "Did you see her?"

"Oh, yeah. Tall, blonde, and muscular," Taler said.

"Pakl came out to the stables," Lise said. "I heard her talking to Ral about taking good care of her horse." She scooted closer, leaned over the table, and lowered her voice. "I found out who she is."

"You mean she's somebody important?" Ange asked.

"As important as you can get without being queen." Lise looked around the table. "She's Hekolatis."

"What?" Taler and Arge reacted in unison.

"Laur's waterfalls." Taler fell back against the padded back of the bench. "That means none of us really has a chance to catch her eye."

"That's not true," Lise said. "I heard princesses sometimes leave Emoria because they never know why someone's interested in them at home. Niko, Hekolatis's birth mother is Nara's sister, and she grew up here in Balderon."

"I knew the sister part but I thought Nara came here from Emoria," Taler said.

"Nara spent many years in Emoria, learning to make swords, and Niko went to visit and, after meeting Hyek, stayed," Lise said. "But they were born here and lived here until they were sixteen or seventeen."

"We were just talking about how Hekolatis must have already broken every heart in Emoria," Ange said.

"So you think she's here to find a life companion?" Taler lowered her voice even more.

"As much as any warrior would admit to it, I'd wager," Lise said.

Taler hit the table with her fist and grinned. "And we thought nothing exciting ever happened in Balderon."


"I CAN'T BELIEVE it," a voice exclaimed from the doorway.

Heko looked over her shoulder from putting her few belongings into the wooden trunk at the end of her pallet.

Taine, on her own pallet, rolled over and sat up.

Heko straightened and turned around. The woman with reddish-blonde hair and soft blue eyes much like her own, laughed and pulled her into a hug.

"Look at you. Not only all grown up but already causing more talk around here than I've heard in ages." The woman held Heko at arms' length. "And now I see why."

Heko scrunched her nose. She forgot to check her face for splattered mud. "Hey, Aunt Nara. Hope you can use a couple more hands in the shop. This is Taine."

Nara turned to Taine. "Well met, Taine."

Taine grinned. "Well met, Nara."

"Welcome to Balderon." Nara spread out her arms. "Not a bad place once you get to know it."

Heko and Taine exchanged glances.

"We . . . uh . . ." Taine bit her lip. "We . . . uh . . . weren't expecting to see . . . uh, so many . . . people."

Nara gazed at them with barely concealed mirth. "Everyone fresh from Emoria has the same reaction. Believe it or not, you'll get used to being around men."

Heko and Taine exchanged skeptical looks.

Nara laughed. "You both must be hungry. I'd be honored if you joined me for the evening meal."

"The honor would be ours," Heko said. "But first, I'd like to get cleaned up." She rubbed her face.

"Of course," Nara said. "I see that Pakl has already sent up the hot water. I'll meet you in the common room."

She grinned as she walked out of the chamber and closed the door behind her.

Taine gave Heko a curious look. "You don't have mud on your face."

"Huh?" Heko looked back from shedding her weapons and boots.

"You don't have mud or blood or food from the midday meal on your face," Taine said. "That's not why people are staring at you."

"There must be something. No one stares at me in Emoria," Heko said. "Except those girls who keep following me around."

"Let me put it this way." Taine cocked her head. "You know how you feel when you watch Jygar spar? That it's like watching the most perfect embodiment of sword work?"

Heko felt a sudden longing for home at the memory of the countless sandmarks she spent watching Jygar wield a sword. "Everything about how she handles a sword is so beautiful that holds you as if under a spell."

"You've got something about you that holds people in a spell," Taine said.

Heko could only stare at her.

"I'm just telling you this so you won't be thinking you've got something on your face all the time."

"I think you got too much sun today." Heko stepped behind the panels that separated the wash area from the rest of the room.


HEKO WAS SO happy to see the sparring pits on the shared roofs of the safe house and blades shop that she smiled. The summer nights were long and, even after two long days on horseback, she needed to feel her sword in her hands more than she needed sleep.

She nodded to the Emorans who had stopped sparring and watched her with intense curiosity. She moved her body and sword through a series of warm-up formations. Her mind calmed and her world settled, and the tensions of the city flow out of her.

A tall, red-haired woman swaggered up to her, swung her sword, and clanged it against Heko's . She held it against Heko's strength.

"We hear you're pretty good." The redhead pulled back the pressure and lowered her sword. She gazed at Heko with cool green eyes. "You hardly ever hit yourself in the head, that is."

Heko flipped her sword. "Is there a point to your observation?"

"We just want to make sure you're good enough to practice on this roof." The redhead sauntered around Heko, making a show of sizing her up.

"And you're going to introduce me to the best warrior in Balderon?" Heko whipped her sword up against the redhead's thrust and twisted the sword from her hands.

The sword clattered on the stone roof. The gathered Emorans stared in stunned silence.

The redhead picked up her sword, turned to Heko, and studied her for a few heartbeats. "All right. Heko, meet Heko, the best warrior in Balderon."

Heko laid the blade on her shoulder. "And will I be introduced to the second best?"

The redhead grinned. "Nohi. Welcome to Balderon, Cousin."

Heko whipped her sword into a salute, then lowered the blade. "Well met, Nohi."

Nohi returned the salute. "Well met, Hekolatis. Are you interested in a sparring partner."

Heko sauntered around Nohi. "I heard you're pretty good. That you rarely hit yourself in the head. Maybe we can work on your slippery fingers."

"You got lucky." Nohi got her blade up in time to stop Heko's lunge. Her sword clattered to the roof again.

The watching Emorans grinned in anticipation.

"It'll be a pleasure learning some of the festival tricks you homeland warriors like to play," Nohi said.

"Festival tricks." Heko gifted them with an impish half smile. "It's only magic if you can't do it yourself."

Nohi grinned. "And they don't call you The Trickster for nothing."

# Chapter 4

"I'D BE HITTING everything but the steel with everyone staring at me like that." Nohi leaned over the service bar in the blades shop and peered through the back entrance into the open-air forge.

Taine looked up from putting a new shipment of swords on a long table in the shop. "She's never aware of anything except what she's supposed to be doing."

They watched Heko for a few heartbeats. She wore a light shirt with the sleeves torn off and her leather leggings. Her arms and shoulders were well-muscled and her flat stomach stuck to the sweat-soaked shirt. She looked born to swing the mallet that flattened the multi-folded steel that would eventually be fashioned into a sword blade. She was indeed focused on her task, taking her turn as four women hammered the glowing metal.

"There's already a lot of speculation about why she's here," Nohi said.

"Is it too hard to believe she just wants to see a bit of the world and be able to walk around without everyone knowing she's a princess?" Taine asked.

Nohi stepped out from behind the bar to help Taine with the swords. "Poor Heko. Too bad she didn't get her nose broken or something during her training."

Taine laughed. "Knowing her luck, it would have made her even more irresistible."

"So she doesn't have the idea of finding a life companion out here away from Emoria?" Nohi asked.

"Is that all anyone around here thinks about?" Taine polished a sword blade with a soft piece of leather.

Nohi gave Taine a sidelong look. "She's not the only one everyone's talking about."

Taine looked up. "What?"

Nohi picked up a sword and flipped it a couple of times. "Heko isn't the only good looking," she looked Taine up and down, "rather rakish stranger who arrived in town."

Taine laughed. "Everyone here really must be starved for diversion."

The rhythmic ringing of the mallets against steel stopped, and Nohi looked out the back doorway. "Oh no."

"What?" Taine put down a sword and went to stand next to Nohi.

"City soldiers," Nohi said. "They can't pass up a chance to tease us."

They got to the doorway just as two women in the dark green uniforms of the soldiers of Balderon walked up to Heko, who lowered her mallet and watched them.

"Looks like another wannabe warrior has come down out of the mountains," a soldier said. She sported a mop of black hair and a battle sash.

The blonde soldier smirked. "Must have washed out of warrior training for being too cute."

"Washed out? I'd wager laughed out." The black-haired soldier ran her eyes over Heko. "Her eyes are too soft and pretty—like a giggly boy's."

The eyes in question flashed a reaction to that. The soldiers laughed.

"So the soft warrior has some backbone after all," the blonde said.

"Either challenge me or get on your way," Heko said. "The metal's going cold."

"Us challenge you?" The black-haired soldier crossed her arms. "We've flung enough insults to get you to throw one of those braids at us."

Heko leaned on the long handle of her mallet and gazed at the soldiers. "You call those insults? If an Emoran warrior got caught uttering such words, she'd be teased for spouting mushy romantic terms of endearment."

The soldiers bristled and glared at Heko.

"How dare you insult our insults." The blonde pulled her sword and leveled it at Heko's throat. Heko looked disinterested. "Soldiers' Lane at dusk. You against the two of us. Sarie and Radle of the Balderon Guard." She sheathed her sword and stomped out of the back alley followed by her companion.

Taine leaned her shoulder against the door jam. "And I was afraid you wouldn't make any new friends here."

Heko shrugged. "They were amiable enough."

The others stared at them with incredulous looks.

"Uh, Cousin," Nohi said. "Challenges don't quite mean the same thing here as in Emoria."

Heko frowned. "Don't they want to fight?"

"Yes," Nohi said. "But they were really insulted. They are truly angry with you."

Heko rubbed her chin. "But they still want to fight."

Nohi gave her a puzzled look. "Yes."

"Then after we fight, and I beat them, I'll apologize for insulting them," Heko said with an impish grin.

The others laughed and relaxed. Nohi gazed at Heko. Having her royal cousin around may prove to be very interesting.


HEKO'S UNEASE AT walking through the city lifted the moment they stepped into an alley off a crowded main road. The noisy atmosphere coming from the far end of the alley crackled with a familiar spark. The feeling blossomed as they strode into a small cobblestone plaza. Smokey open-air taverns sprawled around it in drunken jumbles of tables, chairs, and canopies. Not to mention more drunken guards and warriors than Heko had ever seen in one place.

The last bit of sunlight illuminated the warrior clientele of the taverns. The colors of the uniforms of different cities were mixed with the uniforms of the soldiers of Balderon, including the distinctive brown leather armor of the soldiers from the military compound at Ynit. No man would dare enter this warriors' domain.

Heko and Taine exchanged glances and grinned. This was one place outside the safe house where they could feel comfortable . . . once Heko proved her place among these soldiers.

Heko glanced back at Nohi, Taler, Ange, and Lise. "Like home."

Nohi pushed a clump of hair off her forehead. "Must be an interesting place."

Several other Emorans were already partaking in the ale and lounging in groups around the plaza. Heko frowned as the women stopped their conversations and drinking and stared until it seemed as if all eyes were on her.

The pair of soldiers who had challenged her received encouraging thumps on their backs from their comrades as they walked to the middle of the plaza. Heko glanced at her companions.

Taine clasped her shoulder. "Don't have too much fun." She followed the others to a table of Emorans.

Heko strode to her challengers.

"So, do you want to take us on one at a time or both together?" Radle, the black-haired soldier, asked.

Heko shrugged. "Neither choice is much of a challenge, so it doesn't matter to me."

The soldiers exchanged glances and unsheathed their swords.

"We'll fight you together," Radle said. "We don't want our ale to get too warm."

Heko crossed her arms and waited. The soldiers frowned and lowered their swords.

"We don't *like* our ale to get too warm," Sarie, the blonde, said.

Heko uncrossed her arms and shook them out. The soldiers exchanged uncertain glances.

Radle pointed her sword at Heko. "Are you ready to fight?"

Heko looked down at herself and shrugged. "Yep."

The soldiers circled her and held their swords at the ready.

"Your ale is getting warm," Heko said. "A problem we never have in Emoria."

The soldiers' eyes widened, and they swung their swords. Heko thrust out her hands and grabbed their wrists. Their swords clattered on the cobblestone. Still holding their wrists, she flipped over the space between them. She let go, slung her arms around their necks, and pulled them together.

"Is this ale dark and menacing like the kind we brew in Emoria?" Heko asked. "Or is it the meek and cowardly mice milk that passes for ale in this part of the world?"

The soldiers struggled against her choking hold.

"Ah. You want to fight some more." Heko released them and stepped back.

The soldiers spun around and lunged at her.

Heko ducked under their flying fists, and the soldiers twisted to avoid hitting each other. She rolled away from them, stood, and waited for them to find her.

"Stop playing and fight." Sarie's voice sounded like a frustrated growl.

"What's the fun in that?" Heko stopped a punch to her face and flipped Sarie to the stone ground.

Radle put her arm around Heko's neck from the back. Heko bent forward and flipped Radle over her head. She landed next to Sarie.

Radle and Sarie climbed to their feet and gave Heko a wary look.

Radle straightened and sauntered around Heko. "The fun will be us proving that you only know festival tricks, and you can't fight your way out of a gaggle of ducks." She picked up her sword and laid the blade on her shoulder. "The only wounds from your sword have been from you whacking yourself."

Heko cocked her head. "I recall nicking a duck or two."

She grabbed the hilt over her shoulder and eased her sword from its scabbard.

Sarie picked up her sword. "No more tricks?"

Heko pretended to give it some thought and then nodded. "No more tricks."

The sizable crowd that had swelled with patrons from within the taverns stopped their wagering and sideline comments and waited in silent expectation.

Radle swung her sword, and Heko parried it. Radle attacked from different angles. Heko stopped each with her blade. Sarie stepped in, and Heko countered both blades. Radle and Sarie attacked with greater speed and complexity. Heko relaxed as she deflected their swords, enjoying the workout.

Radle and Sarie came at her at full force and pushed her back to a cluster of watching warriors. Heko stopped both their blades and shoved them back. She picked up a tankard from the table, flipped away from their flying blades, and landed on the table . . . still holding the tankard and not spilling a drop of ale. She took a sip.

"Hmmm. A bit warm but still drinkable." She put the tankard down, flipped over her challengers' heads, and tapped each of them on the shoulder with the flat of her blade.

They spun around in frustration.

"You promised no tricks," Radle said.

Heko gave then an innocent look. "That was a trick?" She thrust her blade forward and whipped the swords from their hands. "Maybe we should discuss the definition of trick. Over a tankard of freshly tapped ale."

Sarie picked up her blade and pointed it at Heko. "You paying?"

Heko jingled her belt pouch and raised an eyebrow. Radle and Sarie exchanged glances and grinned.

NOHI, AS ALWAYS, watched Heko with profound curiosity. Not only was the future Queen of Emoria preparing the forge fire for the day but doing it with earnest diligence. And the night before, Heko had acted like an ordinary Emoran warrior and had every soldier in Balderon wanting to be her friend . . . How did Taine put it? Without even knowing she was doing it, Heko seemed to be able to mold the world around her to fit her view of it.

"You look like you actually enjoy doing that." Nohi walked into the three-sided lean-to that housed the forge. She hated the pre-dawn chore, and the forge helpers took turns getting up to do it.

Heko looked up. "I find it relaxing."

"A dirty, mindless task," Nohi said.

Wielding long metal tongs, Heko pushed and piled the glowing, smoky coals until an orange flame engulfed them. "The task of bringing fire to life from cold lumps of coal."

"Most of us don't have such a philosophical view." Nohi sauntered around the forge. "Of course, most of us wouldn't have the guts to walk into Soldiers' Lane and behave like an Emoran warrior and get away with it."

Heko gave Nohi a puzzled look. "I *am* an Emoran warrior. How else would I act?"

Nohi chuckled. "Those poor soldiers had no idea what you were doing."

"What do you mean?" Heko spread the coals for the second forge fire.

"They don't know Emorans never draw a sword against a foreign soldier until they are attacked—except in battle of course."

Heko frowned. "Why don't they know this? Emorans have lived in foreign cities for a long time."

"For one thing, we never have a reason to fight soldiers who are our allies," Nohi said.

"But what about challenges and sparring?" Heko asked.

"We never spar with soldiers, and the challenges are so rare I can't remember when the last one happened," Nohi said.

Heko raked the coals. "How have you cultivated friendships with the soldiers?"

"Believe it or not," Nohi said, "friendships between warriors can be made without first drawing a weapon."

Heko stared at her with a confused expression. "How?"

Nohi laughed. "We walk into one of the taverns in Soldiers' Lane, order a tankard of ale, and talk to the soldiers."

"Talk." Heko lit a taper from the first fire and set the kindling around the coal aflame. "You've never fought with them. What do you say?"

"Depends," Nohi said. "Sometimes we ask about news we may have heard. Sometimes we ask if the ale is freshly tapped. We may ask a soldier about an unfamiliar sash . . ." She caught Heko's uncomprehending expression. "Those are conversation starters."

Heko's eyes looked inward in thought. "Wouldn't it be easier to challenge them than to think of ways of starting a conversation? After the challenge, you have something to talk about, and it's actually interesting."

Nohi picked up a piece of slag and turned it over in her hands. "Your friend, Taine, didn't seem to have any problems starting conversations with the soldiers last night."

Heko shrugged. "She's a scout."

Nohi gave Heko an amused look. "You had every soldier in Soldiers' Lane trying to start a conversation with you. You didn't seem to have any problem talking to them."

"They asked about my fighting technique," Heko said. "Because they had seen me fight. They didn't have to think of something to talk about."

Nohi cocked her head. "You know, you were pretty clever about how much ale you consumed last night."

Heko looked confused again.

Nohi laughed. "No one noticed you drank maybe one tankard."

Heko shrugged. "I learned the hard way I don't have a head for ale. Everyone was too drunk to notice the tankard of ale in front of me wasn't refilled as often as theirs."

"Besides, they weren't paying attention to your ale." Nohi grinned as Heko tried to maintain an impassive expression while her cheeks turned pink. "Ah. So you aren't completely unaware of your roguish charm."

Heko turned her attention to coaxing flame from the coals.

"I don't see what the problem is," Nohi said. "They don't know you're an Emoran princess."

Heko blinked up at her. "They were only interested because I'm a warrior."

"They were interested because you were the most interesting woman in Soldiers' Lane last night," Nohi said.

"Because they saw me fight," Heko said.

Nohi put her hands on her hips. "I wager you can walk into the tea room across the plaza dressed in plain leathers and no weapons, looking like a common shop hand, and draw the attention of everyone in the establishment."

"No one would give me a second look, even if they bothered with a first look," Heko said.

Nohi shrugged. "Sounds like you want to take me up on my wager."

Heko cocked her head. "I'll do it, if it will put this nonsense to rest once and for all."

"The usual wager around here is a week's pay," Nohi said.

"You get paid more than I do," Heko said.

"You want to make the wager or not?"

Heko stepped away from the forge and brushed her hands on her leathers. "Taine will be witness."

Nohi grinned. "Agreed."

# Chapter 5

"THIS HOT VALLEY air is doing strange things to your brain."
Taine stepped behind the privacy wall that separated the bathing area
from the rest of the room.

"Nohi was the one who made the challenge." Heko was stretched
out on her bed, staring at the ceiling.

"A wager, not a challenge." Taine, now in her sleep shirt, walked
around the wall to her bed and sat on it.

Heko frowned. "A challenge with a wager."

Taine laughed. "I recommend you save some of this week's pay so
you won't starve next week."

"And you think *I've* soaked up too much of this valley heat," Heko
said. "I'm doing this so you'll see that I'm just an ordinary person
when you take away the warrior leathers and the word 'princess' in
front of my name."

Taine grinned. "If you say so." She stretched out on her cot. "So
what do you think about it here?"

"I think I'm starting to get used to it," Heko said.

"Now that we've found Soldiers' Lane," Taine said.

Heko gave her a knowing look. "You just like the attention of all
those soldiers."

Taine propped up on an elbow and faced Heko. "Three of them
actually asked me to come back to their rooms with them last night.
Strangers. I didn't even know their names. I couldn't believe it."

Heko sat up and stared at her. "You can't think they meant . . ."

"I asked Nohi about it," Taine said.

"That explains why she was, all of a sudden, in a bad mood," Heko
said.

Taine scrunched her nose. "What?"

Heko shrugged. "I don't think she was too happy to learn that
those soldiers were interested in getting to know you better."

Taine sat up, cross-legged. "Exactly what are you trying to
say?"

"Nohi's interested in you," Heko said.

"What?"

"Nohi looks at you without trying to be obvious, she mentioned you this morning . . ."

"What did she say?"

Heko gave Taine an amused sidelong look. "She mentioned you just in passing . . ."

"What did she say?" Taine grabbed a rag from the floor, wadded it up, and threw it at Heko.

Heko pulled the rag out the air and grinned. "And isn't it interesting that out of all the Emorans you could have asked about the soldiers' intentions, you chose Nohi."

"She was the first one I saw." Taine scowled. "What did—?"

Heko wadded up the rag. "And it's just a coincidence that you seem to be on the roof when she decides to spar and work on her formations."

"All right. All right." Taine threw up her hands. "I think she's rather interesting. Now what did she say?"

Heko laughed. "She mentioned you had no problem starting up conversations with the soldiers."

Taine frowned. "She noticed enough to mention it?"

"Yep." Heko tossed the rag back to Taine. "Something to think about the next time one of those soldiers invites you to her room."

Taine bit her lip. "So you think she's really interested?"

Heko shrugged. "Why don't you try to kiss her? That's the only way you'll know."

Taine sucked in her breath. "I'm going to have to be really convinced of her interest before I try that. You warriors don't make this any easier you know."

Heko smiled, thanking Laur for that one small blessing.


HEKO SIGHED AS she slumped on the stool behind the service bar in the blades shop. The late afternoon sun filtered through the thick opaque glass of the front window, and a breeze, with the warmth of deep summer on it, blew in from the open doorway.

The blades shop was interesting enough for a quiet activity but her warrior heart shouted for a chance to hold her sword. Even sparring every free moment was not enough. A warrior needed purpose.

The distinctive stomp of soldiers' heavy boots against the plaza cobblestone wafted in on the breeze in the quiet of the afternoon. The pair that filled the doorway immediately lifted her from her funk. She enjoyed talking with Sarie and Radle.

"Greetings, fierce warrior." Sarie grinned as she unsheathed her sword and laid it on the bar. "Think you can fix this?"

Heko studied the broken hand guard. "How'd this happen?"

"Scrubbing out some scum in Lowtown," Sarie said. "They'll come at you with whatever they can get their hands on. Fortunately, my hand wasn't anywhere near the sword when it was axed."

Heko gave her a puzzled look.

"One of the thieves whacked it out of my hand with a skillet." Sarie shook her hand. "That really stung."

"Skillet?"

Radle looked up from the sword she was inspecting. "Favored weapon of the underclass."

"Such a strange world you live in," Heko muttered as she took the sword to the forge.

Nara, flushed and sweating from the fire, looked up from the final touches to an exquisite blade.

"Hand guard." Heko held the sword up.

"Put it there. Should take a half sandmark." Nara nodded at a workbench. "Taler, stoke the fire."

Heko stepped back into the shop and stopped and gazed at the soldiers who were silhouetted in the sunlight that spilled in through the doorway as they looked at the swords on display. She took in their well-worn uniforms, their casual confidence, their air of satisfaction . . . They were warriors with a purpose. She shook away the envy that washed over her.

"It'll take a half sandmark," she said.

Sarie grinned. "Gives us a chance to look at some of these new swords."

"Wish I could afford this one." Radle sighed as she whipped a sword with a silver hilt in a few formations.

"I've never seen that move before," Heko said.

Radle chuckled. "The Balderon bash?"

"The what?" Heko got caught up in their good humor.

"Ah, it seems your education in weaponry has missed some very important innovations in the art of swordplay." Sarie sauntered around Heko with her hands clasped behind her back. "The Balderon bash is essential for the skilled warrior's scabbard of tricks. Observe."

She picked up a sword and went after Radle with a flurry of attacks. Radle turned sideways, and Sarie launched into the Balderon bash that ended with whacking Radle in the behind.

Heko doubled over with laughter.

"You'd be surprised how handy that move can be at times," Sarie said.

Heko wiped her eyes. "Are there any more moves like that missing from my obviously very limited scabbard of tricks?"

"Are you familiar with the Artocian choke, the Ingoran slice, or the ever useful Ynit flame out?" Radle demonstrated each one.

Heko laughed so hard she held her sides and gasped for air.

"Every city has made their own contribution to our fighting skills," Sarie said. "Every city except Emor."

Heko hung her head in mock shame. "I'm afraid we've been remiss in our duty to the soldiers of the Southern Territories."

"You know, the problem is, you Emorans keep to yourselves too much," Sarie said. "Your warriors don't even go to Ynit to serve in the Federation army."

"We love our country too much to leave it for long," Heko said. "If there were some other way of serving without the six year commitment . . ."

"You can always join the auxiliary guard." Sarie picked up another sword and looked down its length.

Heko frowned. "The what?"

"The Auxies," Sarie said. "Part-time soldiers. Called upon for special duties. They usually get travel duties—mostly guarding and escorting rich families or minor royals. Us regulars are stretched too thin in our duties for that kind of work. They also help with crowd control, patrolling festivals, and the like . . . Many are retired soldiers, some are local young women who passed our weapons tests."

"Anyone can join?" Heko worked to keep down a growing excitement. "You don't have to be from Balderon?"

Sarie gave the sword a couple of flips. "We've got Auxies from all over. Many settled here for one reason or another."

Heko frowned. "Why would they live somewhere that wasn't their home?"

Sarie shrugged. "Balderon has become their home."

"But it's not where they grew up. They aren't surrounded by the people or the places they grew up with. Where they are a part of the life, the history . . ." Heko couldn't find the right words to remove Sarie and Radle's blank looks.

"I don't think the rest of us have quite as strong an attachment to our birthplaces as Emorans do," Radle said.

"So, how does one join?" Heko asked.

Sarie cocked her head at Heko. "Life in a blades shop not exciting enough for you?"

"I'm used to spending my days being a warrior," Heko said.

"All you have to do is show up to Auxie training," Sarie said. "They see what you can do. Train you on what you're lacking and show you everything you need to know about being a soldier of Balderon."

Heko nodded as she wound the idea through her mind. "I think I might want to give it a try."

HEKO EXAMINED HER reflection in the weather-worn mirror the warriors used to study their fighting form and practice their stony expressions.

The brown leather was not too dark or light and was just lived in enough to match any worn by the shopkeepers on the plaza. She looked, to her eyes, ordinary. With her unruly hair that couldn't look any other way but tousled, with her muscular body hidden by the loose leathers, she looked . . . unremarkable.

Except. She frowned as she studied herself . . . something about her didn't look like an ordinary shopkeeper. She still looked like a strong, solid warrior, even with her muscles hidden. She flexed her shoulders and experimented with slumping them . . . making them look natural. Ordinary.

When she got just the right slump, she nodded in satisfaction.

"Are you finished, already?" Taine asked.

"I think so." Heko straightened at the mocking impatience in Taine's voice. She carefully restored her slump.

Taine and Nohi exchanged amused glances.

"Let's go, so we can get a table," Nohi said. "We've got to time it so the place is almost full so you have as big an audience as possible."

Heko rolled her eyes. "Not an audience. The only reason they'll even glance my way will be because of you and Taine in your Emoran leathers and weapons."

"We're wearing these because you asked us to prove your point," Taine said. "But you're going to walk in first, and we're going to peek in through the windows to see the patron's reactions."

Heko shook her head. "You two are crazy. I'm going to walk in and be so invisible a server will probably bump into me and spill a pot of tea on my leathers."

Nohi turned to Taine. "Want to help me spend my winnings?"

Heko rolled her eyes and trotted down the outside steps to the alley below, followed by Taine and Nohi.

The evening air held a clarity that only happened after a cleansing rain shower and appeared to be irresistible to city folk who spent too much time inside. The people gathered in the plaza stopped in mid-word and mid-action to stare at Heko.

She turned to Nohi and Taine who were smirking. "They're staring at you, not me."

"Glad we didn't wager on how long you would remember to slump," Taine said.

Nohi grinned. "These folk are probably wondering why an Emoran warrior is dressed like a Balderon shopkeeper."

Heko shook her head and strode ahead of them.

Taine stifled her laugh as they joined Heko, who was gazing into the window of the tea shop. Her amusement turned to puzzlement. "What's wrong?"

Heko blinked at her. "Uh . . . uh . . ." She swallowed as she watched the tables full of people. Enjoying their tea and conversations.

Nohi looked through the window and then at Heko. "What?"

"Uh." Heko took a deep breath, and felt her cheeks warm. She cursed that her fair skin showed the slightest bit of embarrassment.

Nohi crossed her arms, her eyes dancing with amusement. "I don't think I've ever seen an Emoran warrior blush before."

"You've never seen one kissed in public," Taine said.

Heko bowed her head to hide her cheeks.

Nohi grimaced. "I've heard about that tradition."

"If you ever go to Emoria to earn your braid, you'll learn about it first hand," Taine said.

Nohi cleared her throat and looked as uncomfortable as Heko felt. "I think I can spend my life very well without a braid."

Taine laughed and then frowned at Heko. "Now what's wrong?"

"I've . . . uh . . ." Heko looked at her feet. "I've never been in a place like this. It looks so . . . neat. Everyone is so . . . uh . . . well behaved."

"You're dressed like a shopkeeper. You'll fit right in," Nohi said. "At least that's what you're hoping you'll do."

Heko worked the idea in with the reason she was there in the first place. She was a warrior, not afraid of anything. Why was she suddenly afraid of walking into an establishment that sold tea, of all things? Why did she feel she didn't belong in the shop, and everyone would know it the moment she crossed the threshold?

She turned to Nohi. "Have you ever been in here before?"

"Many times," Nohi said. "They serve the best spiced tea in town outside the safe house, of course. That's why it's always so busy."

Heko nodded and gave her a sheepish look. "Sorry. I never knew I had such a problem with trying new things."

"It's that warrior training," Taine said. "They make you so focused you ignore everything else in the world."

"And some of us stay more focused than others," Heko said.

"You must have glanced around a little to have made friends with a scout," Nohi said.

Heko grinned at Taine. "We became friends when we found the same hiding place when we were six."

"And what were you hiding from?" Nohi asked, amused.

Heko scrunched her nose at the memory. "A bunch of girls wanting to put flowers in our hair during the Festival of Flowers."

Nohi hooted a laugh. "I've heard about that tradition, too. The moment a girl starts warrior or scout training all the other girls go out of their way to embarrass them."

Taine sighed. "We can't wait to spend our summers in the barracks away from the city."

"I'm kind of glad I didn't have to put up with all that while growing up," Nohi said.

"It must be odd growing up Emoran, yet only knowing of our everyday life and traditions from a distance," Heko said.

"We took care of that problem by creating our own everyday life and traditions," Nohi said. "Some we share with all the Outlander Emorans. Others specific to the cities we live in."

"And that everyday life includes visiting local tea shops." Heko realized her nerves had settled down. Sometimes talking things out helped. "I think I'm ready to go in." She straightened and Taine and Nohi tried to hide their grins.

Heko went to the opened doorway and stepped inside. The establishment was much larger than it looked from the outside, and the windows allowed for the evening sun to keep it light longer without lamps. The patrons facing the door glanced up from habit. Their glances turned to admiring gazes, causing their tablemates to turn around and others to crane their necks to see what was so interesting in the direction of the door.

Heko frowned and looked behind her, expecting to see Taine and Nohi, but they were outside watching through the windows.

"There's a nice table in the back."

Heko turned to a young woman with an eager-to-please smile.

"That would be fine," Nohi said as she entered with Taine.

"This way." The young woman smiled at Heko as if she had been the one who had spoken.

A confounded Heko glanced back at Nohi and Taine who exchanged amused looks. They gave her a little push to follow the young woman to a table.

# Chapter 6

JYGAR STOPPED AT the place where the alley opened onto the plaza known as Soldiers' Lane. Now she understood why the local Emorans liked to spend their evenings there. The atmosphere was very Emoran-like but bolder and rougher around the edges.

She sauntered onto the plaza and scanned the inhabitants of the tables sprawled outside the taverns. All she had to find was the table with the toughest, roughest warriors . . . ah there. She grinned. Heko looked like she was in Laur's Paradise surrounded by those battle-hardened soldiers and warriors.

Jygar approached the table to hear what had captured everyone's riveted attention. A silver-haired warrior with long aging muscles and a spectacular scar across her face was recounting how she got that scar. Jygar noted how Heko seemed to be drinking in the battle blows and the descriptions of exotic adventure. The old warrior finished the story and the appreciative audience cheered and thumped their tankards against the tables.

Jygar signaled a server for ale and caught Heko's eye.

Heko looked surprised to see her and a bit apprehensive as she climbed off the bench and squeezed around the tightly-packed patrons. "Jygar. Good to see you."

"Good to see you, too." Jygar turned to the server who approached with her ale. She took the tankard and slipped a coin into the server's hand. "You look well. You seem to be fitting in here in Balderon."

Heko shrugged. "It took a while to get used to."

"You seemed to have made friends with the local soldiers," Jygar said.

"Yeah." Heko looked at her feet. "I can talk to them and just hang out with them, like I used to do with the warriors back in Emoria."

"So you left home to experience the world and found something to do that reminds you of home?" Jygar gave her an indulgent smile and nodded at an empty bench.

Heko followed her to the bench and sank down onto it. "It's different. These warriors have to deal with threats and criminals all the time. Being a warrior is not only who they are, it's their job."

"So you've decided you want to give it a try for a while," Jygar said.

"It's a way I can be a warrior and see something of how the world outside of Emoria works," Heko said.

Jygar nodded. "Hyek is open to the idea. Niko is familiar with the auxiliary guard here and knows what kind of work they're usually called upon to do. Not much warrioring as far I can tell."

"It's an opportunity to learn about these people and this culture," Heko said. "I'll be able to get out and about more, see more of this city and maybe other parts of the Southern Territories."

Jygar cocked her head and gave Heko an amused look. "Shop life not exciting enough for you?"

"It's interesting enough, and I'm learning a lot. But I just get restless." Heko looked out at the darkening plaza. Several soldiers from different cities were showing off their sword technique. "I need to feel . . . I don't know. Useful."

"And you don't feel useful in the blades shop?" Jygar watched as a Southern Territories soldier demonstrated a very interesting move.

"I feel useful enough. They always need strong arms to hammer the metal," Heko said. "It's just I feel more useful as a warrior."

Jygar laughed. "I understand completely."

"So I'm allowed to join the Auxies?" Heko asked.

"All Hyek asks is you wear your braids." Heko nodded agreement. "And you don't go out of your way to get in harm's way."

Heko frowned. "Sometimes this job can be dangerous."

"She understands that," Jygar said. "What she means is don't do anything beyond your duty that will put you in harm's way. You must never forget you're the Emoran heir, and the regular soldiers are getting paid to do the really dangerous, heroic stuff."

Heko chuckled. "From what I can tell, Auxies are never near anything dangerous or heroic."

"There's always a first time," Jygar said. "Just be careful and use good judgment when faced with situations that can be potentially dangerous."

"I'll be careful," Heko said. "I'd never do anything to cause my mothers undue concern."

Jygar nodded and raised her tankard to Heko. "You've always been a good daughter."

HEKO SIGHED AS the Kender sisters insisted on checking the last three back alleys for shops that carried tea cozies. The small town of Quinler was nestled in the western foothills of the Phytian Mountains, and Heko couldn't stop from gazing at the mountains and thinking of Emoria.

The sisters' stone mason business was successful enough for them to own nice homes and support their families. Heko couldn't understand why they spent their extra time and money on, of all things, tea cozies.

"Oh, there's one." Jader Kender pointed to a display of tea settings—including a rather ugly tea cozy—in a window and clasped her hands with excited anticipation as she entered the tiny shop.

"I just knew we'd find something in this part of town," Jena Kender said as she followed her sister.

Heko tried not to roll her eyes as she bent through the narrow low door. The sisters had already cornered the shopkeeper on the types of tea cozies he carried. With barely enough room for three people to move, much less four, Heko remained just outside the doorway.

She had been assigned to act as bodyguard for the Kender sisters several times in the eight moons she had been a part of the Auxies. At least the sisters traveled quite a bit to the towns around Balderon. Unfortunately, most of the trips were for pleasure, and the Kenders' great passion was tea cozies. They carried quite a bit of silver to buy additions to their collection, making it necessary to hire a guard.

Merchants were now requesting her by name, something Heko didn't understand until she had asked Sulti, the Master Coordinator of the Auxies. Sulti had belly laughed at the question. She explained that Heko looked and acted a bit more refined than the other soldiers. She was always polite and respectful, and didn't leer or make passes at any of the daughters of the household. This last caused Heko to straighten in indignation. Warriors never made the first move—in Emoria at least. Things were so much different in the outside world.

So she spent the last moons learning many valuable things about merchants, including how they wasted their time and money. She also learned the inner workings of the city guards—knowledge she knew would be invaluable when she became queen.

All in all, she was glad she decided to join the Auxies but wished she had the occasional opportunity to earn her wage. She never had the chance to protect her charges from potential danger with a menacing glare much less with her sword—another reason, Sulti had told her, the merchants wanted her as a guard. A guard was a signal that a merchant carried a large amount of silver, and many thieves took it as a challenge to get to a greater reward than usual. For some reason, thieves never tried to rob the merchants Heko guarded.

"This has been such a good shopping trip," Jader said as she and Jena approached the door.

Heko backed away to let them through.

"And the sun came out to help take away the chill," Jena said as they rambled back to the main street.

Heko couldn't understand why everyone thought the winter was so cold. It rarely got cold enough to snow. The people of Balderon would never be able to survive a spring, much less a winter, in Emoria.

"Heko, people are staring at you again." Jader laughed with her sister.

Heko's tendency to attract attention had become something of an amusement for the merchants she guarded, and she almost quit and ran back to Emoria when she found out merchants fought to have her as their guard at important events. Having a tall, strong, good-looking guard as a part of an entourage turned out to be an attention-getting asset for them. She was always a bit bemused when a merchant would offer her an outrageous wage to become a part of the household staff.

Heko pulled from her belt the shapeless dark green beret that was a part of the Balderon soldier uniform and put it on.

"I hear you're going to fetch our niece back from Artocia," Jena said.

Heko nodded. "I leave the day after next."

"Artocia is a nice city." Jader waited for Heko to open the door to their coach and put down the decorated box that acted as a step.

"The University is quite spectacular," Jena added as Heko helped both into the coach, put the box onto the back, and climbed in after them.

As much as Heko hungered for knowledge, she never had much use for learning from books and scrolls. She preferred learning through experience. She had a hard time envisioning a University as being remotely interesting, and she reserved terms like spectacular for a good battle.

"Have you ever been to Artocia?" Jader asked.

Heko settled into the seat opposite the sisters. "No, I haven't."

"Emorans live there," Jena said. "We've had more than one business meeting at the Artocia safe house."

Heko nodded. The people she guarded always tried to make her talk about her people and Emoria. They seemed to have an unnatural fascination for her country as an all-woman society, and some of the questions they asked were enough to make her cheeks redden. Outsiders were a lot more casual about some things than Emorans.

"You know, sister, we ought to pay a visit to Emoria," Jena said. "In the summer, when it's warm in the mountains."

"What a wonderful idea." Jader turned to Heko, who tried to keep from looking alarmed. "We've always heard that your city is made of white stone, and that the stonework is unique and breathtaking."

"The stone in that part of the mountains is white," Heko said. "The stone work is different from here—"

"And we'd be the talk of Balderon to have tea cozies from Emoria," Jena said.

Heko hoped they didn't see her full-out alarm. "We, uh, don't sell anything we make except swords and knives and ale."

"Really?" Jena seemed genuinely surprised. "Certainly you wouldn't deny a visitor's silver in one of your shops."

Heko blinked at her. "I mean we don't sell anything to each other in Emoria. And we don't sell anything but swords and knives and ale to outsiders."

The sisters gaped at her. Heko knew they'd never understand something so against their merchant sensibility.

"But how do you get your food and clothing and all the things you need to live?" Jader asked.

Heko cocked her head. "We grow, make, and hunt everything we need."

"But how do you distribute everything?" Jena asked.

"We put it in the communal stores, and when we need something we go there," Heko said. "Also when we no longer need something, and it's still perfectly usable, we take it to the stores so someone else can use it."

The sisters exchanged intrigued looks.

"Now I'm even more curious about Emoria." Jader's eyes glistened with excitement.

Heko spent the trip back to Balderon convincing them, as tactfully as possible, that they didn't want to visit Emoria. Hyek would kill her if curious visitors started arriving at the borders.

HEKO PEERED OUT of the coach window as they rounded a low hill. The landscape changed to scrubby sand. She had heard of the desert but could never envision it. She certainly never imagined endless flats of sand and strange-looking plants.

The winter sun made the world cleaner and brighter than even the mountains after spring rains. The land was bizarre and alien, but Heko was drawn to it. She wished she had the chance to explore it.

The coach left the dirt side track and clattered onto the main road that ran from the east coast to the west coast of the Southern Territories. They were close to the Sea to the south—closer than Heko had ever been to a body of water larger than a lake. She was glad she had studied a map before the trip.

She stared in amazement at the road made of stone slabs wide enough for coaches to pass each other. She arched her body out the window to look ahead at the endless road on the flat sand.

She squinted at the wavy air hovering above the sand in the distance. Something long and dark seemed to span the horizon. As the coach lumbered closer, the line transformed into a wall—a high wall with buildings the color of sand peeking up behind it.

"Ynit," she breathed in awe.

She spent the rest of the journey with her head out the window, unable to take her eyes off the largest city she had ever seen growing ever larger until the coach slowed and rattled through the gate. She looked up as they passed under the ramparts that had to be at least ten paces wide. And the wall itself . . . she tried to fathom something that tall built by a force other than a deity's hand.

The coach continued to what looked to be the heart of the city. Heko's senses were overwhelmed by the bright adobe and the warmth and the noise of the open-air markets that sprawled everywhere she looked. The people were sun-darkened, and wore light but sturdy looking clothes. The markets had bursts of color from stacks of patterned cloth and rolled-down bags of fruits and spices she had never seen before.

The coach finally stopped on the edge of a plaza in front of a stable. Heko carefully rose and stepped from the coach without hitting her head. Her knees almost buckled, and she grabbed the door bar. She shook her legs out and took a few steps until she trusted them not to give way.

"The safe house is over there." Haren—a servant of the House of Ponadin, the owner of the coach—jumped from his place atop the coach and pointed across the plaza. "We'll be leaving in a sandmark."

Heko nodded and left the young man to exchange the exhausted horses for a fresh team.

A pair of women in the distinctive uniform of the soldiers of the Southern Territory sauntered past and gave her a casual once-over she had grown used to from soldiers. They reminded her that the military compound was somewhere in this city. She really wanted to see the legendary fortress but didn't dare wander from the plaza. The surrounding seemingly endless streets and buildings that spilled into the expansive plaza intimidated her more than she'd ever admit to anyone.

She strode to the blue door with a sword and bow etched on it and rapped against the hard wood. A small panel slid open and closed. The door opened onto the usual narrow corridor found at the entrance of safe houses.

The silver-haired woman looked Heko up and down and raised an eyebrow at the Balderon uniform and the Emoran warrior braid dangling from her belt.

"Come in. I'm Trera, the proprietor."

Heko stepped inside the corridor—dim compared to the bright desert sun.

"From Balderon, I see."

Heko nodded. "I'm Heko. My aunt runs the blades shop in Balderon."

Trera's other eyebrow went up. "If you want to pretend to be from Balderon, then you'd better work on losing your mountain accent."

"I grew up in Emoria." Heko followed Trera into the common room. The familiarity of it was a welcomed relief after the intimidating foreignness outside the door. Hyek would be less than pleased to know that she decided not to wear her princess braid but any reprimand would be better than endless attention and questions from other Emorans.

"And you decided to settle in Balderon?" Trera smiled when all eyes in the half-full room stared at Heko.

"Not settle." Heko fought the urge to turn and run away from all the eyes on her. "Just live there for a while."

An older woman with a bearing that told Heko she was of high standing in the safe house community beckoned to Trera.

Trera nodded and led Heko to a table in the back of the chamber.

"Please join me," the woman said. "I'm always interested in outside news."

Heko settled onto the bench across from the woman.

"Tea or ale?" Trera asked.

"Tea, please," Heko said.

Trera signaled a server and walked away.

"I'm Gargis. Proprietor of the blades shop," the woman said.

"Heko."

Gargis studied Heko as the server put a plate of food and tea on the table. "Is that your full name or a nickname?"

Heko stopped her fork halfway to her mouth.

Gargis laughed. "Don't worry. I don't expect an answer. I've recently been to Emoria and happen to know a prominent citizen is currently out and about."

Heko let out a relieved sigh. "Thank you for not making a fuss. It's nice to be able to go about without drawing attention."

Gargis glanced around and suppressed an amused grin. "It's a bit odd to see an Emoran in a Balderon city soldier uniform here in Ynit."

"I'm on my way to Artocia to pick up the daughter of a merchant and take her back to Balderon," Heko said.

Gargis wrinkled her nose. "The constant threat of kidnapping has made those young women too spoiled."

"That's something I don't understand." Heko put down her fork. "Their mothers' are strong and competent, like women should be. Yet their daughters act weak and . . . and . . . I don't even have words for it. I've never seen women act like that before."

"Let me see if I can explain," Gargis said. "In the last ten or fifteen years, since our uneasy truce with the Kuntics, the number of kidnappings and robberies and murders have increased so much it's not safe to have money or political prominence anymore. These girls grew up being sheltered—they know no other way to live. They've been denied the opportunity to develop into strong, independent women."

"But certainly their mothers must have seen what was happening and tried to do something to help them," Heko said.

"They did what they could." Gargis leaned over the table and captured Heko's eyes. "But it's hard to teach being strong and assertive and intelligent in one breath and in the next breath, warn their daughters to be wary of strangers, be cautious every time they step outdoors, and be vigilant of bold thieves that may invade their very homes." Gargis sat back and took a swallow of ale. "I fear for the generation of girls that have grown up under this reign of fear."

Heko frowned as she wound the idea through her mind. "I can't help but think, if we Emorans had been more in tuned to the rest of the world and more open to giving help when needed, we may have been able to do something to help stop this rise of criminal activity."

Gargis took another sip of her ale and gave Heko an appraising look. "I think Emoria's going to be an interesting place when you have some say in how it's run."

# Chapter 7

A FULL DAY after leaving the safe house in Ynit, Heko climbed out of the coach and touched the cobblestone streets of Artocia with numb feet at the end of numb legs. Never had she sat in one place for so long—even with the stops for the evening and morning meal, the jarring ride was much too long.

She gazed up at the huge stone buildings around her with astonished awe.

"These are her trunks." Haren motioned to several trunks in a long line of trunks on the closed-trimmed grass bordering the road.

Artocian guards stood every five paces or so around the jumble of possessions that belonged to the well-off students who, Heko surmised, inhabited the low, many-winged building in front of them. Haren had told her the University felt the students were easier to guard if kept in one place.

"I have to go get feed and water for the horses." Haren trotted off to a small building where two roads crossed.

The trunks in question bore the insignia of the House of Ponadin.

Heko grabbed the handle of one and gave it a tug. "Does she study rocks?"

The closest guard laughed. She had the bronze skin of many of the inhabitants of Ynit and eyes so dark they were almost black. "You probably don't want to know what these students think they can't live without. Let me give you a hand."

"Thanks."

"We're always seeing new guards." The guard took the other handle of the trunk, and they lifted onto the back of the coach.

"It's not that tough of a job." Heko grabbed a smaller trunk.

The guard gathered several bulging leather bags. "You're luckier than most. Zandar is more levelheaded than a lot of them."

Heko gave her a wry look. "Yet she's had many guards."

"Only because they haven't been able to do their job." The guard spread out her hands. "Protect Zandar from thieves."

"Haren told me they've been robbed when they've stopped on the way back," Heko said.

"If you know how to handle that fancy sword, you'll have a job for life." The guard nodded at the sword on Heko's back.

Heko grinned. "I can hold my own."

They pushed against the trap door to get it closed, and Heko used all her strength to secure the latch.

Heko straightened and took a recovering breath. "She's just going to be home for two fortnights."

The guard laughed. "Maybe I'll see you on the trip back."

"I'll be back," Heko shrugged a shoulder, "if I do my job properly."

Haren trotted down the road toward them. "All packed?"

"Yep." Heko put out her arm to the guard. "Thanks for your help."

The guard grasped her arm. "My pleasure."

"No one ever leaves until after the midday meal," Haren said. "Some kind of ages-old tradition. But be thankful for it, or else we'd not be able to eat until we reached Caterle."

"Is the safe house close by?" Heko looked around.

"Not this time," Haren said. "The closest place is over there. It's where the regular students eat."

"Regular?"

Haren lifted his chin at the building behind them. "The ones who can't afford to eat in their own private hall."

"The ones who don't have to worry about thieves and kidnappers," Heko said.

Haren nodded. "But the good news is, the food is cheap and hasn't killed me yet." He headed for a cluster of buildings at the end of the road.

Heko looked around amazed as they walked across the close-trimmed lawn. She had halfway expected the University to look like a little city. Never did she envision an open and pleasant place with expanses of grass and cobblestone plazas between the buildings. The buildings, although made from the same brooding stones, were of different sizes and shapes and seemed to have distinct personalities.

Haren nodded at the building to their left. "That's the History building. It has a circular hall with murals that show the history of the Southern Territories. The building over there is the Science building. It has an incredible museum."

"Museum?" Heko frowned at the unfamiliar word.

"A place where they put on display the things the scientists have collected over the centuries," Haren cheerfully explained. "Things like the skeletons of dragons, crystal rocks from the mountains, fossils."

"And people want to see these things?" Heko asked.

"Oh, yeah. Some of the stuff in there is amazing."

They circled around a low building. Young women and a few young men were gathered in clusters on a pleasant square that boasted stone benches and a fountain. Even from a distance, Heko felt suddenly stupid. They all looked so . . . intelligent. As they passed by, she picked up bits of the conversations. They were speaking the common language but she couldn't begin to understand what any of them were talking about.

"Whoa. Things are looking up around here," a woman said.

Heko blinked at a group of young women in front of her. All were gazing at her with unabashed admiration. She cursed the blood rising to her cheeks and focused her attention on the cobblestone.

"You can guard my body any time you want, good-looking," the bold young woman said. The others giggled as Heko hurried past them. "Well, what do you know, a shy guard."

"Ignore them," Haren said. "They like to tease the guards."

They stepped through the doorway into a noisy, large chamber filled with tables and students, professors, and quite a few guards. The conversations filling the space didn't sound like any Heko had ever heard before. More of those unfamiliar words peppered discussions of books and writers and artists and music and history and . . . She tried not to notice that many in the room had stopped in mid-sentence and mid-bite to stare at her.

Haren sat at a table filled with several other household servants and guards. Heko slid in next to a guard and gratefully accepted the plate of food and tea from one of the many servers dashing around the chamber.

Under normal circumstances, she would have been interested in the lively conversation at the table. She had a fascination with the different social classes of the Southern Territories, and the servants were endlessly entertaining in their astute observations of the families they served. But she couldn't shake the blow to the core of her very being that all the certainties of her world had been shattered.

Heko was going to be queen of a country. Looked upon to make important decisions. How could anyone ever think she had enough knowledge to do that? Confusion washed over her. She knew as much as anyone in Emoria—was even considered intelligent. She certainly took the time to think things through to find the best possible solutions to problems and to make the best decisions.

She sighed as she munched the bland, but filling stew. Thinking wasn't the problem. The problem was what she had in her mind to work with. She wondered if the scholars and archivists in Emoria knew all the knowledge the students around her knew. If they did, why weren't they the rulers?

She finished her meal in more confusion than when she started. If she had never visited this University she would have become queen and ruled—like all the queens before her—blissfully ignorant of this knowledge. *But now that I know about it . . .*

"Time to get back to the coaches," a woman said. She wore the gaudy city uniform of Ingor.

Heko followed the others out of the hall and across the green. This time she looked around with curiosity, trying to envision so much knowledge that it had to be contained in huge buildings made of impenetrable stone.

Haren checked over the coach to make sure it was still in good repair.

Heko leaned against the vehicle, watching the students trickle out of the several doorways of the building and going to their coaches.

They had a different look to them than the students she had seen in the mess hall. Their clothing was of better quality and less worn looking. Not necessarily flashier or brighter in color, like the clothes their sisters who chose not to attend the University wore back in Balderon—these daughters of merchants didn't want to draw attention to themselves. Gargis had told her these women were the hope of the next generation because they resented having to live a sheltered life. Most had more than a bit of rebellion in them.

A tall, young woman strode out of a side door. She wore a simple tunic and leggings of green and brown leather and her black hair was cut short. Something about her gave off a strength and confidence that Heko found lacking in the daughters of the merchant class she had encountered so far.

Heko realized the young woman was headed in her direction. Worse, she realized she was staring at this student. She quickly looked at her feet. She prided herself on never exhibiting open admiration of another woman. No warrior ever had a reason to tease her about that. On the other hand, she had never really had a strong inclination to be caught in the kind of spellbound stare women gave her all the time.

"Haren," the young woman said.

Heko looked up at her pleasing voice and tried not to stare as the young woman talked to Haren as he removed the feedbags from the horses. She widened her eyes when the woman turned and walked to the door of the coach. Heko blinked, opened the door, and started to the back for the step box.

"Don't bother." The student waved. "Glad to see Mother hired a new guard. I really don't want to experience being robbed again. I'm Zandar, by the way."

Heko cleared her dry throat. "Heko."

Zandar gave Heko a quick up and down look. "At least you look like you know which end of a sword to point at someone." She climbed into the coach.

Heko gave her head a shake, got into the coach, and settled across from Zandar, who had already pulled a book from her pack and was bent over it.

The coach lurched and clattered out of the University grounds and the city of Artocia.

Heko studied her hands while sneaking peeks at Zandar, who seemed to be unaware of anything around her except the book. She realized Zandar hadn't paid any undue attention to her. Just treated her like any other guard. Like a normal, ordinary person.

As the sandmarks passed, she was relieved Zandar wasn't attempting small talk or sneaking curious looks at her. But she also had an odd longing to hear Zandar's voice again and find out something about her. She frowned at the idea. She was sure she wouldn't be able to exchange more than three words with a University student.

Zandar got to the last page of the book, closed it, and looked as if she didn't quite want to let the words go yet. As she slipped the book into her pack she gave Heko a quick, friendly smile. Then she adjusted some cushions in the corner of her seat, nestled into them, and dozed off.

Heko was still coping with the smile and the hint of a twinkle in Zandar's blue eyes. She couldn't help but watch Zandar as she slept, and when the coach rattled into the courtyard of the House of Ponadin, the long day-and-a-half trip felt like it ended much too soon.

HEKO LEANED AGAINST the doorjamb of her chamber. "So are you planning a Winterfest joining?"

Taine turned from putting her clean leathers into the trunk at the end of her bed. "Am I going to endure endless teasing for the rest of my life?"

Heko grinned as she sauntered into the room and dropped her pack onto her bed. "I go away for three days, and the first thing I hear when I step in the door is my blood sister is going to be joined to my cousin. I figured it's worth a couple of decades of teasing, at least."

Taine stood and shrugged. "What can I say?"

"So I take it you finally kissed her," Heko said.

"Oh yeah," Taine said. "It was pretty ale-soaked but it was worth it."

Heko laughed. "I hope the discussion about a joining wasn't as ale-soaked."

Taine smiled. "No. It was a long, serious, sober discussion. We especially talked about where we'll live."

Heko looked up from putting her pack into her trunk. "I hope you decided to spend time in Emoria."

"We decided to split our time between here and Emoria," Taine said.

"I'm glad you had the good sense to fall for a warrior. Much better than those acolytes and . . . and archivists." Heko grinned and hoped Taine didn't catch her faltering.

"Speaking of." Taine gave Heko a sidelong look. "How was the trip to Artocia? Did you get to see Ynit? Is it really surrounded by sand."

Heko laughed. "Come on. I'll tell you all about it over a tankard."

"Best offer I've had all day."

"That must mean you haven't seen Nohi yet today." Heko ducked as Taine took a swipe at her.

"You're in a good mood for someone who just spent three days in a coach." Taine followed Heko out the door and down the short corridor.

Heko shrugged. "I like seeing new places."

"I'd go crazy cooped up all that time," Taine said.

"It took a bit getting used to." Heko led the way to a back table in the common room.

"Master of understatement." Taine sat on the bench and signaled Lise for ale. "Of course you had company on the way back."

Heko kicked herself for not coming up with a quick, flippant response. "Uh, yeah."

Taine cocked her head. "That bad, huh?"

"She spent most of the trip reading or sleeping," Heko said.

"Reading?" Taine accepted a tankard from Lise.

Lise made a comical face at the word, put Heko's tankard in front of her, and sauntered away.

"She's a student." Heko took a long sip of ale.

Taine raised an eyebrow at Heko's half-filled tankard. "So was she at least as interesting to look at as the scenery?"

Heko blinked at her. "What?"

Taine laughed. "You'd better thank Laur I'm not a warrior."

"Huh?" Heko gave her a puzzled look.

"I've seen you warriors tease each other for less than your distraction," Taine said.

Heko tried to look shocked, but knew it was true. She would tease another warrior for even a hint of how she was acting. "It's nothing. She barely looked at me much less talked."

"Barely looked at you?" Taine scrunched her nose.

"I was just a guard," Heko said. "There to guard her."

"What do you mean barely looked at you?"

Heko sighed. "She just looked at me when she had something to say, except . . ."

"Except what?" Taine looked like she wanted to strangle Heko.

"Except when she finished one of the books, she looked at me and smiled."

"Ah, now we're getting somewhere."

"A friendly smile," Heko said. "A brief friendly smile."

Taine scratched her head. "As hard as it is for us to understand, there are some women who prefer men. Although I haven't noticed that small fact stops them from staring at you."

"I've spent the last eight months guarding her aunts," Heko said. "Her mother has been trying to fix her up with several successful merchants. I've learned that being attracted to women opens up the chance of creating merchant alliances."

Taine took a long sip of ale. "Then you have a chance." She grinned at Heko's exasperated look.

"Even if I was interested, I have no chance," Heko said.

"Why not? An Emoran princess beats a merchant any day of the week," Taine said.

Heko stared into her tankard, wondering where the strange sadness overtaking her came from. Somehow, meeting Zandar made the realization she had in Artocia all the more painful. She gave Taine a sheepish look and shrugged. "Maybe."

Taine nodded and grinned as she signaled for another ale.

# Chapter 8

NOT LOOKING BORED was an important skill for a future queen, and Heko was getting plenty of practice. The one part of her job she liked the least was guarding the silly daughters of merchants at what they called Evening Socials. She had to do several of these events to numb her disgust at young women behaving so . . . so . . . she still didn't have any words to describe such unwomanly behavior. Weak, frivolous, giddy, shrill, babbling. And they acted this way for sandmarks at a time.

She exchanged long-suffering looks with Bris, the guard on the other side of the kitchen door. The girls always hired one of the nice eateries for the evening. Heko did feel sorry for them. This was the only way they could have an evening meal out and socialize without maintaining a constant vigil and not having guards at each shoulder. No one should have to live with that kind of fear.

"Oh no," several voices groaned, and heads turned toward the entrance. Gathered in the doorway were a group of young women in well-tailored but subdued clothes—compared to the bright colors that filled the room. Heko straightened and looked at Bris.

"It's all right." Bris nodded her chin at the door. "The Unies have decided to invade their sisters' party."

"Unies?" Heko asked.

"The sisters home from the University," Bris said. "It's kind of a tradition and is really all in good fun, no matter the complaining and protesting from the homebies."

"Homebies." Heko grinned. She loved the endless nicknames the people of Balderon were fond of using.

"They all grew up very close," Bris said. "And they've had to create their entertainment any way they could." She grinned. "No matter how strange."

The students strode in and stopped before they got to the tables. A young woman who looked a bit older than the others stepped in front of the group and crossed her arms. "We wanted to eat at our favorite Inn and what do we find? Our dear sisters have decided to take it over.

But we didn't despair. We knew they had just forgotten we were in town and forgot to mention this little gathering to us."

The young women at the tables, keeping back smiles and giggles, solemnly nodded in agreement.

"So we thought," the bold student said.

The students grinned and worked their way around the crowded tables, greeting old friends and family and finding places to sit. Subdued colors mixing with bright colors at least made the group easier to look at.

Heko relaxed and continued her observation of this new twist in the endlessly entertaining behavior of Balderon's merchant class. A second smaller group of students straggled in. She caught herself staring—again.

Zandar stood in the doorway and then went to a table where Heko saw several beckoning hands. Heko noticed that, like the other students, Zandar's smile was both amiable and indulgent, like she was there more out of tradition or maybe as just a diversion from being cooped up at home.

Heko snapped her attention back to the door. Several young women in the colors of the different merchant houses strolled in. She turned to Bris.

"The young, single merchants like to crash these events." Bris grinned. "It's a way they can flirt with whoever has caught their eye without any parents lurking around."

Heko worked on that idea for a few heartbeats as she watched the merchants move among the tables. So this social activity was really some kind of courtship ritual. From what she could tell, the merchants weren't the only ones engaging in flirtatious behavior.

She frowned and scanned the tables, where more women were now standing and milling around rather than sitting. Zandar, holding a mug of spiced tea, stood in a cluster of other students. Compared to the boisterous activity around them, they looked to be engaged in a calm, thoughtful discussion. Heko couldn't stop a sigh of relief— her initial impression that Zandar was there just for something to do seemed to be correct.

A merchant with cropped dark hair and medium height but with enough of an arrogant swagger to make up for it, sauntered up behind Zandar and whispered in her ear. Zander stiffened, obviously not happy about the woman intruding on her conversation with her friends.

Heko narrowed her eyes as an unexpected anger rose up from deep within her.

The woman looked like the type who never read the subtle polite signals that said "leave me alone" as meaning anything more than a challenge, and she continued to try to get Zandar's attention away from her friends.

"I'd love the chance to toss that one out," Bris said.

Heko blinked at her. "What?"

"The one bothering Zandar." Bris lifted her chin at the merchant. "Her name is Brandle. She spent the last few years building her House of Brandle and seducing every willing young woman in town. Zandar caught her eye about a year ago, and she's been pursuing her ever since. Rumor has it Brandle and Zandar's mother have almost reached an agreement to create an alliance between their Houses and a joining between Zandar and Brandle."

"Surely Zandar has some say in this." Heko couldn't imagine a mother doing such a thing to a daughter.

"Not until she's reached the age of consent."

Heko gazed at Zandar and frowned. "How old is she?"

Bris shrugged. "She's in her third year at the University. I'd say about nineteen."

"What's the age of consent here?"

"Twenty-one." Bris gave Heko a curious look. "What is it in Emoria?"

"Eighteen," Heko said.

"Then Zandar would have been better off being from Emoria," Bris said.

"If this were Emoria." Heko clenched and unclenched her fists. "Brandle would be facing a dozen warriors politely suggesting she leave Zandar alone."

Bris laughed. "Unfortunately, we guards can't do anything unless Zandar signals she needs help. Let's just say it would be very embarrassing for Brandle if she had to be escorted out of here by guards."

Heko gave Brandle a cold look. "Maybe a little embarrassment is what she needs."

Bris shrugged. "Because Zandar is underage, it would only make her mother and Brandle angry with her."

"It just doesn't seem fair," Heko said. "She's older than I am. How can it be that I'll be of legal age before she is? She attends the University and lives away from home most of the year. Doesn't her intelligence and independence mean anything?"

"Not here." Bris gave Heko a sympathetic look. "I hear it used to be better when the merchants didn't have to worry about getting robbed or kidnapped. It's hard times all around."

Heko returned her attention to Zandar, who looked like she was trying to ignore Brandle as unobtrusively as possible. Zandar's friends were also trying to encourage Brandle to leave them to their conversation. Heko couldn't keep down her anger and indignation at Brandle's disrespectful behavior.

"I can't believe you'd rather talk about some silly battle that took place a hundred years ago than share some wine with me." Brandle's voice rose above the noise.

Heko glanced at Bris, who also kept an eye on that side of the chamber but didn't seem to hear Brandle. Heko thanked Laur and all her acolytes for her gift of keen hearing.

Unfortunately, Zandar refused to match Brandle's rising voice and murmured her response. Whatever she said only added fuel to Brandle's irritation. Heko watched and prayed for Brandle to cross whatever imaginary line was considered inappropriate behavior in this strange society.

"I'll tell you one thing." Brandle's tense voice touched Heko's ears. "This pretending you're not interested act is not cute anymore."

Heko's level of respect for Zandar soared when she turned around, crossed her arms, and gave Brandle a look that said, "Do I look like I care?"

Brandle, obviously not used to that kind of reaction, looked momentarily nonplussed. She then straightened and said something in a low voice. She bowed to Zandar and her friends and casually sauntered away to join another cluster of women.

Heko raised an eyebrow at this.

"She knows when to retreat, I'll give her that," Bris said. "But I think it's only a matter of time before her ego finally gets the better of her, and she does something regrettable—for her that is."

"I would be very pleased if she did that when I'm around," Heko said.

Bris grinned. "You and about every other guard who has had to put up with her through the years."


HEKO FOLLOWED NOHI through the blades shop into the forge, around the anvils and fire pits and out into the alley to a pile of ingot bars. The morning was dark and cold and the clouds promised a dreary gray once the sun rose.

"Nara wants four," Nohi said.

Heko, lost in thought, blinked at her.

Nohi put her hands on her hips. "Am I going to have a reason to start teasing you because of a certain merchant's daughter?"

Heko sighed. "It's not that." She picked up two ingots.

Nohi picked up her two. "Then what is it?"

Heko followed Nohi back into the forge and piled her ingots next to an anvil. "Why hasn't anyone done anything to stop this rise in criminal activity?"

Nohi looked up from preparing the fire pit. "Good question. I think the problem just kind of crept up on everyone, and when they realized it was major, it was too big to control."

Heko thought about this as she prepared the second fire. When it was burning to her satisfaction she walked to the edge of the forge and stared at the building across the alley. "I don't accept that. They could have done something but it was easier to take the silver of those who needed the most protection and hire guards for them rather than use those same guards to supplement the local city soldiers in controlling the problem."

Nohi gazed at Heko in amazement. "I think that royal blood just flowed into your brain. The problem is, the Southern Territories are ruled by a Federation Council, which in turn is controlled by those who have the loudest voices and the biggest piles of silver. The merchants have no problem with paying for guards to protect themselves and their households but don't want to contribute to a common fund that would increase the number of soldiers to protect everyone else."

"But what about chasing down these criminals and getting rid of them?" Heko faced Nohi. "They're not phantoms. They're real, and they live somewhere. They're obviously organized, so I suspect they live in well-guarded hideouts somewhere . . ."

"Again, that takes silver no one is interested in spending." Nohi pushed on the bellows to get the flame going. "I agree with everything you say, and Emorans don't have these problems because we know how to take care of them—before they become problems. But we don't even have a say in the Federation Council because we chose to remain a sovereign country and are only bound to the Southern Territories through treaty agreements."

Heko went to an anvil and ran her fingers over the hammered surface. "But we put in those treaties the option to join the Federation Council when we felt ready."

Nohi gave her a knowing look. "I think Hyek needs more of a reason than her daughter's desire to pound the heads of all the thieves and kidnappers in the Southern Territories."

"That's what I don't understand," Heko said. "Why doesn't everyone have the desire to pound the heads of all these criminals that have essentially taken the Southern Territories hostage?"

"Because everybody thinks it's someone else's job, and no one will step up and say, it's my job, and I'll do what I can to get it done," Nohi said. "And this person can't be just anyone. She has to be someone people will listen to. Someone who has what it takes to get the job done."

Heko sank down onto a short log that passed for a seat in the forge. "There must be someone who has the right qualifications."

Nohi nodded thoughtfully. "There may be. And maybe she just needs a nudge in the right direction. Or maybe she isn't interested in bringing attention to herself, more content with being an ordinary citizen."

Heko stared at Nohi. "What are you saying?"

"You know what I'm saying," Nohi said. "You can't go around lamenting how someone who can actually do something about it won't get involved when you, yourself, have turned away from your birthright so you can act like a regular person."

Heko was dumbstruck. She wove the idea through her mind as Nohi finished the tasks in the forge.

"You're right." Heko stood up and followed Nohi into the shop. "Except I'm not the right person for the job."

Nohi picked up a couple of leather rags and tossed one to Heko. "Why not?"

Heko snatched the rag out of the air. "Why not? For one thing, I'm an Emoran. Who else, besides other Emorans know me, much less would listen to me?"

"So you think someone from Balderon or Ynit or Rihnon wouldn't have the same problem?" Nohi asked. "No one can claim the whole of the Southern Territories as their home territory. This person has to be able to transcend territories."

"Someone like a great general," Heko said.

"The great generals from the last war are either dead or too old," Nohi said. "Maybe that's why nothing has been done about this. They were even too old when the Kuntician treaty was signed."

"Wencer used to say that war makes heroes and peace makes politicians," Heko said.

"Isn't that the truth." Nohi arranged several new swords in the window display.

Heko picked up a sword and polished it. "I'm going to have to think about all this for a while."

Nohi grinned. "Maybe you can get that student you're sweet on to help you."

Heko scowled, flipped the sword, and pointed it at Nohi. "Let's make a pact. You don't tease me about Zandar, and I won't tease you about Taine. Agreed?"

Nohi crossed her arms and pretended to consider the offer. "Agreed."

Heko grinned and resumed polishing the sword. She was accompanying Zandar back to Artocia in just three days.


HEKO WOKE WITH a start. She straightened as best she could with the gentle rocking of the coach. She saw that Zandar had closed her book, and was watching her in a kind of nothing-else-to-do way.

"What's that?" Zandar nodded at Heko's belt.

Heko looked down at herself. "A braid."

Zandar frowned. "As in an Emoran braid?"

Heko nodded.

"Did you win it in a wager or something?" Zandar asked.

"I trained for it," Heko said.

Zandar cocked her head and looked at Heko as if for the first time. "You're an Emoran? Like actually from Emoria?"

Heko nodded.

Zandar sat up, eyes sparkling with interest. "I read that each braid has a meaning. What's your braid for?"

"For passing the initiation to become a warrior," Heko said.

"So you're really a warrior?" Zandar said. "Not just trained by the soldiers to know enough to be a part of the auxiliary guard?"

"I'm really a warrior," Heko said.

"So why aren't you warrioring, instead of guarding spoiled merchants and their offspring?" Zandar's eyes twinkled with a pleasing impishness.

"There isn't much opportunity to be a warrior these days." Heko looked down at her hands.

"If I'm not being too nosy, why are you in Balderon?" Zandar asked. "My subject at the University is history with an emphasis in military history, so I'm interested in the behavior of warriors. And Emoria is such a mystery to scholars."

Heko stared at her in astonishment. "You know military history?"

Zandar grinned. "My question first."

Heko was caught off guard by the sudden wave of charm flowing off of Zandar and amazed that she was talking to her in an ordinary conversational way about something interesting. "Many Emorans like to spend a few years outside of Emoria, seeing what the rest of the world is like."

"I'd have picked some place more interesting than Balderon," Zandar said.

"Anywhere outside of Emoria is new and interesting to us," Heko said.

"But why did you pick Balderon?"

"My aunt runs the blades shop there," Heko said. "And it's only two days on horseback from Emoria."

"Really?" Zandar sat up straight and perched on the edge of the seat. "Emoria isn't marked on any maps. We just know it's up in the mountains somewhere."

"It's impossible for anyone to find us," Heko shrugged, "unless we let them."

"So why did you decide to join the Auxies?"

"Because I wanted to feel a little more useful than hammering metal and tending the shop," Heko said.

Zandar laughed. "I won't embarrass you by asking if you feel more useful."

Heko studied the floor and shrugged. "At least I get to travel and learn about the world a bit."

"After studying about the armies of the past," Zandar stared out the window and then rested her gaze on Heko, "I can't help but feel sad that we don't know what to do with all that skill and training in peacetime."

Heko sucked in her breath and stared dumbstruck at Zandar. She didn't want to move or think or do anything to wake her up from this miraculous dream.

"Take this nonsense the Auxies have to do." Zandar, caught up in her own idea, didn't seem to notice her effect on Heko. "Why aren't we doing something to stop the crime instead of putting up with it?"

Heko realized her jaw had fallen open and closed it. She tried to remember how to produce sounds through her vocal chords.

"Of course, those who control what soldiers can and cannot do have no understanding of the power a peacetime force can have." Zandar leaned forward with her elbows on her knees. Her body tense with excitement. "Reducing the Southern Territories army to one regiment and then spreading that to five remote outposts, with the largest number of soldiers remaining in Ynit was based more on greedy Council members wanting to budget for their own pet projects than for any consideration of what such a reduction may do to our continual defenses. They point to the city soldiers as the best type of peacetime military force. Please. Some Council member conjured that reasoning out of thin air."

Heko's mouth drifted open again as she stared spellbound at Zandar.

"Anyone with a whisper of knowledge about military strategy knows our current system is the equivalent to an engraved invitation for an invasion." Zandar crossed her arms and plopped against the cushioned back of the seat.

Heko struggled to say something . . . anything. "Uh . . ."

Zandar noticed Heko's wide-eyed expression and gave her a sheepish look. "Sorry for the lecture. I tend to get focused on things that really interest me or really ticks me off and run on about them a bit too much."

"Uh, no problem," Heko stammered out, both relieved and astonished by the apology.

The coach slowed, signaling that they had arrived in Artocia.

"This was fun," Zandar said. "If you're the guard who comes to get me at the end of term, maybe we can talk a bit more about your warrior training in Emoria."

Her dazzling smile almost stopped Heko's heart, and she knew her life was in peril if she witnessed another smile, but she also knew she would die if she never saw it again.

# Chapter 9

"I HAVE TO admit it's nice to get out in the woods again." Taine stooped to inspect a snapped twig and a partial footprint half hidden by dried leaves.

"Says the woman who's going to be joined to a city Emoran." Heko grinned. "Which way?"

Taine stood and scanned the tangle of paths leading out of a patch of flattened vegetation that looked like a favorite sleeping spot for deer. "That way. They're not being too careful."

"They have no reason to be," Heko said. "No one has tried to stop them in ten years."

"If Nohi hadn't told me about your ideas before you went to Artocia, I'd be convinced you were doing this to capture the attentions of a certain student." Taine followed the narrow path out of the clearing and into a woods.

"I'd be doing this anyway," Heko said. "But it's nice to know someone else has the same ideas."

"Especially the someone you'd like to get to know better." Taine danced out of the way of Heko's playful swipe. "What if you aren't chosen to go get her from Artocia?"

Heko chuckled. "Her mother is so pleased with my services she's requested I be assigned as needed."

"You do know if you figure out how to stop these criminals, the merchants won't have any more need for guards." Taine looked back at Heko. "Which means you'll have to find some other way to see Zandar."

"I have the feeling there's more to all this than bands of thieves and kidnappers," Heko said. "Anyway, right now I'm just gathering information about them."

"So you can talk it out with, let's see, a military historian." Taine smirked at Heko's exasperated look. "Nohi may not be allowed to tease you, but I can make up for it."

Heko slumped and stuck her hands into the belt.

Taine frowned. "Hey. I'm not teasing you that much, am I?"

Heko shrugged. "It's not that. It's . . . it's not like Emoria where everyone knows each other, and everyone knows when a warrior is interested in them. I mean, that's what the teasing is about. If it's not true then the warrior denies it but if it's true, word gets out. The woman she's interested in knows to make the first move, if she's interested."

Taine sat down on a stump. "I guess that means you're going to have to do something to let her know."

Heko stared at her. "I couldn't. I mean I wouldn't know what to do." She gave her head a shake. "It's not possible. Warriors just don't do that. At least we don't in Emoria."

"Maybe you should have a chat with some of the guards you work with." Taine stood and continued into the forest.

Heko ran a hand through her hair and followed Taine. "I think I will."

Taine stopped and turned to Heko. "She really has caught your eye, hasn't she."

Heko nodded. "Yes. She has."

Taine clasped Heko's arm and gave it a squeeze. "Then she must be a pretty remarkable woman."

Heko sighed. "I hope I have a chance to find out."

"You will." Taine faced ahead and scanned the clearing. "There's a line of bluffs behind those trees."

"We haven't run into any sentries or patrols," Heko said. "They must be further away. Maybe on the other side of those bluffs."

"Shall we practice our stealth skills?"

Heko grinned. "That way?"

"Are you sure you're not a scout?" Taine chuckled as they ghosted through the trees, skirted the clearing, and found a fissure in the rock. They slithered up the tight, uneven stone, well hidden from the surrounding trees.

Heko peeked between the rocks perched on top of the bluff. She shimmied up to behind a nearby boulder. Taine slithered up beside her. They studied the boulder-strewn landscape.

Taine raised a questioning eyebrow. Heko lifted her chin in the direction of several large rocks and held up two fingers.

Taine indicated a possible route with her finger. Heko nodded, and they stayed close to the edge of the bluff as they circled to get a better view of the pair of men who stood so still and quiet they had to be sentries. They paused behind a tall pillar with ancient carvings on it.

Heko studied the carvings and then looked around. They seemed to be on a plateau rising up in the middle of the valley. From where they stood, the center of the plateau looked like ruins of some kind. Her nostrils twitched at the aroma of stew. If they were cooking, where was the smoke? It should have been visible in the clear, cooler air above the valley floor.

She signaled for them to follow the bluff edge.

They rounded the plateau and stooped behind a pillar. The ruins looked as if they'd been recently rebuilt along the edge facing away from Balderon, and the smoke funneled out of the north wall. The Kuntics were the only other people besides Emorans who knew how to live undetected in bluffs and caves. They inhabited the northeastern side of the Phytians in much the same way Emorans lived on the southwestern side.

Heko led the way to another carved pillar on the north edge of the plateau. She took one peek below and dropped to her stomach. Taine, behind her, hit the ground and snaked up next to her. They could only stare at the scene below them.

"Laur's waterfalls," Taine breathed.

The valley was filled with ruins of what must have once been a great city. Some of the smaller buildings had been rebuilt with stone, but many of the new structures were of wood with the ruins as a foundation. This wasn't a makeshift town of thieves. This was a well-organized military outpost. The perfect staging point for an invasion from the north.

"This has been here a long time," Heko said. "Why hasn't anyone found them?"

Taine grinned. "Sounds like the kind of thing a military historian likes to explore."

Heko sighed. "She comes home for the spring festival. In the meantime we try to learn as much as we can about these ruins."

Taine frowned. "The ruins?"

Heko glanced at her. "Maybe there's something about these ruins that keeps the local people away."

"What if they try something soon?" Taine nodded at the ruins.

Heko studied the buildings and the people bustling about. Their clothing was Kuntian, and many were in their distinctive black uniforms. "They won't try anything until the main army arrives."

"And how will we know when that happens?"

Heko cocked her head at Taine. "When the crime all but stops."

"Why?"

"To create a false sense of security." Heko arched her neck to get a better look at what several Kuntians were doing on a long workbench. They were hammering metal plates into thick armor. "My guess is the crime will stop maybe two or three weeks before the army moves into position here."

"These are Kuntics not Emorans, maybe they do things differently," Taine said.

"I'll ask the military historian about the war with the Kuntics." Heko just hoped she could muster the courage to do more than answer Zandar's questions. Maybe asking questions would let Zandar know that she was interested in her. She sighed. Life outside Emoria was so complicated.

"I HATE THE spring festival." Zandar plopped down in the coach. Heko climbed in and closed the door. "That's why I leave Artocia just in time to arrive for the first day."

Heko settled on the seat and gave her a blank look.

"Don't you have a spring festival in Emoria?" Zandar asked. "No wait. You have the Festival of Flowers." She sighed and rocked with the coach as it lurched forward. "Same idea in Balderon, except we wear matching tokens."

Heko stared at Zandar in shocked surprise.

"The tradition in Balderon is for the braver of a pair to ask the other to the spring festival no later than three days before the festival." Zandar pushed back into the seat and crossed her legs. "So the best way of avoiding that little ritual is to not be around for it."

Heko frowned in puzzlement.

"My mother doesn't understand my passion for history," Zandar said. "She can't imagine a scholar or a teacher living a happy and satisfied life. She can't imagine anyone not wanting to make piles of silver for a living. She thinks I'm going to come to my senses when I've finished my studies, and then not have the skills to be a merchant. So she's encouraging every young, single, and let's not forget successful merchant to try to court me." She rolled her eyes.

Heko tried not to look concerned that more than one merchant was interested in Zandar.

"I have nothing against finding a life partner. But I prefer to find one myself. Someone I actually like." She looked at Heko. "Oh. This is making you uncomfortable. I'm sorry. I've read about Emoran warriors and their courtship rituals."

"Read?"

"I wanted to do some research before picking your brain about Emoria's warrior culture," Zandar said. "I found a small section of scrolls and books in the University Archives that, I think, give a nice overview of Emoran society and history."

Heko was puzzled again. And she wasn't happy with the change of subject. "So none of these suitors can bother you during the spring festival?"

"Oh, they can bother me all right." Zandar chuckled. "They just can't pretend to be with me in a courting sort of way. So no one bothers women who go solo to the Festival of Flowers?"

Heko straightened, indignant at the idea. "No one bothers women in that way in Emoria. Any warrior would stop such acts of dishonor."

Zandar cocked her head. "Would you like to accompany me to the spring festival?"

Heko stared in shocked astonishment.

Zandar laughed. "Sorry. I was just testing your reaction. Besides, it's too late for me to ask anyone. But really, would you have a problem with being my guard during the festival? I don't like to do a lot of the events, but it's fun to walk around and see the decorations and, of course, I love the games."

"Games?"

"Competitions in athletic ability and warrior skills," Zandar said. "I'm surprised you're not trying out for any of them."

Heko shrugged. "I didn't know about them."

"I can't believe no one told you about them." Zandar looked Heko over. "You look like you could be a strong competitor with the sword."

"There's a sword competition?" Heko tried not to let her rising excitement show.

Zandar gave her an impish look. "If you're my guard, I can sponsor you in the games if you want to compete. My mother won't let me go without a guard, and I may as well be with someone I can actually talk to."

"I'm not much of a talker." Heko looked at her hands.

"You may not be much of a talker but you're a great conversationalist. You know when to ask the right questions." Zandar smiled. "But you sometimes forget to answer them."

Heko's heart stopped as Zandar's smile penetrated her soul. She struggled to maintain a passive expression and to breathe. "Yes."

"Good," Zandar said. "Now that we have that settled. I can now do some primary source research."

Heko gave her a blank look.

"Ask you questions about Emoran warriors."

Heko decided that Zandar's gentle laugh was even better than her smile.

HEKO WALKED INTO the kitchen just as Idren the cook finished preparing the fire for the day. The sun barely peeked over the horizon, and most of the safe house inhabitants were still asleep.

She was exhausted and hungry. All she wanted was a nice, quiet meal after three days in a coach and sitting across from Zandar for half of that time.

"Eat up and get some sleep." Idren gave her a plate of bread and eggs and a mug of spiced tea.

"Yes, ma'am." Heko grinned as she went into the deserted common room and sat at a table against the wall. She gathered eggs onto her fork, frowned, and looked at the stairs along the back wall. Footfalls in the corridor on the upper floor had a distinctive rhythm that could only belong to Taine.

"Ah ha." Taine ran down the steps and dodged around tables and chairs. She grinned as she disappeared down the corridor to the kitchen and then reappeared with a plate of food and a large mug of spiced tea. She sat down across from Heko, looking ready to burst.

Heko munched the crusty bread.

"Am I going to have to threaten you with teasing?" Taine asked.

Heko sighed. "We talked."

"That's good." Taine gathered eggs onto her fork.

Heko looked up. "She knows about our . . . our courting rituals. I mean warrior courting rituals."

Taine put down her fork. "Really? How?"

"She read about them," Heko said. "When she was doing research, so she'd know what to ask me about being an Emoran warrior."

Taine frowned. "If she could read it all in a book, why did she need to ask you about it?"

"Something about doing primary research," Heko said.

Taine grinned. "I think she just wants to get to know you better."

Heko shoveled food onto her fork. "I don't know. There were a lot of things she didn't know about. She asked for a lot of details. She said the books gave only overviews and sketches."

"What?"

"Those were the words she used." Heko waved her fork. "She explained that no one had really done primary research in Emoria, and most of what's in the books are from secondhand sources—people who have never been there and only heard stories about it."

"I can imagine how accurate a lot of that is."

"That's why she's asking me questions. She wants to write an accurate view of Emoran warriors taken from a primary source. That's me." Heko put her fork down without taking a bite. "She's interested in me as a subject of study."

"But that doesn't mean she's not interested in you in other ways." Taine pulled a small metal token in the shape of a crossed sword and scout's dagger from her belt pouch. "They have some similar traditions around here. Instead of a flower bracer, courting couples wear tokens to their spring festival. Nohi forged a pair of these."

Heko picked up the token and studied the delicate metal work. "She's good."

Taine grinned and took the token from Heko. "Maybe next year you'll go to the festival with Zandar."

Heko stopped in mid-reach to her mug. "I . . . uh . . . uh . . ."

"What?"

"I'm accompanying her as her guard." Heko grabbed her mug and took a deep drink.

"Her mother must really like you," Taine said.

"Uh . . . uh . . ." Heko felt her cheeks get warm.

"You know you blush too much for a respectable warrior." Taine grinned in amusement.

"Zandar asked me if I'd be her guard at the festival," Heko said to her plate of food.

Taine whooped and hit the table.

"It doesn't mean anything," Heko said. "She just wants to be there with someone she can talk to. Someone who shares her interest in warriors and military history."

"So she's going alone?" Taine asked.

"She avoids being asked by arriving in Balderon right before the festival starts," Heko said.

Taine nodded. "The three-day rule. Kind of an odd tradition but very convenient in this case. So she's not interested in that merchant?"

"She said she's not interested in any of the merchants her mother has been trying to fix her up with." Heko pushed around her eggs with her fork. "Did you know they can still pursue her at the festival?"

"Pursue her?"

"Try to make her interested in them by following her around, by trying to engage in conversation," Heko said.

"Like what happened at that gathering?" Taine asked. "But surely in public and especially at a token festival they leave her alone when she refuses their attentions."

"That's just it." Heko pushed down her indignation at women behaving in such a dishonorable way. "They just keep on bothering her. She said she had to miss the games, which is her favorite part, last year because those merchants wouldn't leave her alone."

"But what about her guard?" Taine asked. "Wait. You told me. They can't do anything unless asked, and publicly humiliating a merchant would just get her mother mad at her."

"Yeah." Heko sighed. "As much as I want to spend the next three days in her company, I don't know how much I can take of watching those women bother her without doing something that would get me expelled from the Auxies, not to mention Balderon."

"And get your mothers angry with you," Taine added.

Heko put down her fork and gazed at Taine. "I'm not ready to go back to Emoria."

"Not when things are just getting interesting," Taine said. "Between Zandar and the Kuntics, you've found enough to keep your interest for quite a while."

"Yeah," Heko said. "More than I really wanted."

"I don't know." Taine rubbed her chin. "You found someone who has never been moon faced over you and treats you like a normal human being. And you found a potential army to practice your warrior skills on. Sounds perfect to me."

"It'd be perfect in Emoria," Heko said. "Here, it's just frustrating."

# Chapter 10

HEKO LOOKED AT herself in the small mirror in her room. The few sandmarks sleep, combined with some dozing on the coach, was enough to refresh her, and she looked alert enough. She frowned and tried to comb her tousled hair but it continued to misbehave.

"Paying attention to how you look?" Nohi leaned against the doorjamb.

Heko scowled at Nohi's reflection and backed away from the mirror. She smoothed down her uniform and tied her braid to her belt.

"Seriously," Nohi said. "It's not easy falling for an outsider. But it happens with happy endings."

"I don't think she's interested in me in that way," Heko said.

"We never know," Nohi said.

"She's never looked at me like . . . like others do." Heko gazed at the floor.

"Isn't that what you wanted?" Nohi asked.

"Yeah." Heko frowned. "But . . . I guess I didn't think it all the way through."

Nohi laughed. "What would you have done if she had reacted to you the way others do?"

"I don't know." Heko bent down and brushed some dirt from her boots. "I saw her first, and I was the one who did the staring."

Nohi smiled and clasped Heko on the shoulder. "She enjoys your company. That's a start."

Heko nodded. "I thank Laur for that."


HEKO DODGED COACHES and clusters of cheerful people in festive dress as she strode down the road known as merchants' row. The lavish homes of the more successful merchants sat behind high walls and elaborate iron gates. She stopped in front of the House of Ponadin and smoothed down her tunic as the gatekeeper pulled open one side of the gate.

"Good morning, Heko." Mondor grinned as Heko stepped onto

the smooth stone slabs of the coach lane that circled up to the front door of wood inlaid with the Ponadin crest—an eagle perched on a rainbow. The stone slabs also followed the wall around the house to the inner courtyard.

"Good morning, Mondor," Heko said.

Mondor clasped her on the shoulder. "We're all happy Zandor can go to the festival this year."

Heko frowned a little. She still hadn't figured out the complex relationship between the servants and the houses they served. "I'm glad I can give her the opportunity."

"Well, have fun." Mondor pushed the gate shut.

Heko followed the coach lane to the side of the house. She admired the trimmed bushes and riot of flowers in beds arranged in patterns on the lawn. She liked that the city dwellers still tried to surround themselves with a bit of the country.

She walked through the arched entrance to the courtyard. A corridor that connected the front to the back of the house ran through the arc over her head.

"Hey, Heko." Haren was walking a pair of horses to the coach in the middle of the courtyard.

"Hey, Haren."

"I was happy to hear you were guarding Zandar today." He stopped to settle the horses. "She had to miss the Games last year, and spent every night of the festival listening to old Rewner recount the events. He's the only one of the household staff who gets to see all the Games because he's Ponadin's personal assistant."

Heko frowned at the idea of Zandar having to experience something secondhand just because certain merchants didn't know the meaning of the word "no."

"Ah, Heko," came a voice behind her.

Heko turned around. Ponadin, a tall and slender woman with gray in her dark hair, was an older version of Zandar, but with an elegant dignity that felt to Heko to be more practiced than natural. She wore what Heko had learned was the more casual showing of a House's colors. Her tunic and leggings were tailored-cut but loose enough to be comfortable. The Ponadin black and gold were rather playfully streaked on the tunic.

"Thank you for agreeing to guard Zandar," Ponadin said. "I can't understand what's so important in Artocia that prevents her from returning to Balderon in time for one of her many suitors to ask her to the festival."

She walked to the coach and waited for Haren to open the door and put the box step down for her.

"She ought to be out in a bit," Ponadin added over her shoulder as she climbed into the coach.

Haren rolled his eyes at Heko as he closed the door and put the box step on the back of the coach.

Heko grinned. She was glad Emoria didn't have any sort of class system, but it was entertaining to see one in action—especially one that didn't include intense oppression of the underclasses.

She wandered around the courtyard and finally settled, cross-legged, under a small tree that seemed to sprout from the cobblestone itself. She studied the facade of the two-story building with its overly ornate stonework and oversized balconies. The calls and flutters of the birds nesting in the courtyard played with the muted sounds of clanking metal and chattering voices from the opened doorway in one corner of the yard and with the occasional laughter and talking from the opened windows on the upper floor.

She realized she knew very little about the House of Ponadin. She didn't even know if Ponadin had other children or was still mated to Zandar's father, or if he had been used just to father children. The whole mating issue seemed to be confounded by the desire to have children. If life companions of the same sex wanted children, they had to mate with a member of the opposite sex.

Heko shuddered at the thought. The body was sacred, only to be given in love strong enough for a lifetime commitment. The idea of having to be unfaithful to have a child left a trail of disgust in her proper Emoran sensibility. All they had to do was worship the right deities . . . She gave her head a vigorous shake. It was best not to think about it.

A small boy who looked strikingly like Zandar ran into the courtyard. Heko stared in shock. A male with Zandar's characteristics shook something deep within her. The whole idea of males and females sharing the same blood was an abstraction for her, and she struggled not to feel repulsed by it in the face of this blatant example.

"Zeck," a familiar voice called from inside. A moment later, Zandar walked into the courtyard, dressed in the same kind of well-cut but subdued leathers she had worn when she crashed the evening social. "You'll have to wait for Mother to come back."

"Why can't I go to the festival with you?" Zeck scowled and scrambled for a soft leather ball near the wall.

"Because you have to go with Mother." Zandar caught the ball and tossed it back to Zeck.

"That's not a reason," Zeck said.

"It's the only reason I have," Zandar said.

Heko stood up, catching Zeck's attention.

"Are you really an Emoran warrior?" Zeck asked.

"Yes." Heko brushed off her uniform and walked to Zeck, who arched his neck to look up at her.

"You're taller than Zandar, and she's tall." He drew out the last word.

"A little taller, yes," Heko said.

"Are all Emoran warriors as tall as you are?" Zeck asked.

"Some are. What makes a warrior comes from her skills and desire to be a warrior, not her size." Heko glanced up and got caught in Zandar's delighted smile.

Zandar stepped forward. "Zeck, this is Heko. Heko, meet my brother, Zeck."

"Well met, Zeck." Heko bowed her head.

Zeck gave Zandar a puzzled look.

"That's an Emoran formal greeting," Zandar said.

Zeck nodded and with an earnest expression bowed his head. "Well met, Heko."

"I'm pleased to meet you, Zeck," Heko said.

Zeck cocked his head at Heko. "Are you from a merchant family?"

Heko frowned. "No."

"It's just you're so . . . so polite and speak so . . . clearly," Zeck said. "Like a merchant."

"Emorans don't have the same kind of class distinctions we have, Zeck," Zandar said.

Heko shrugged. "I'm like everyone else in Emoria."

"Don't you have a queen? We're studying the different countries in the Southern Territories right now, and Emoria is the only country that still has a mon . . . monarchy. That means royalty," Zeck said, proudly.

"Yes, we have a queen." Heko concentrated on keeping her

voice steady and matter-of-fact. "Emoran royalty is not raised any differently than any other Emoran."

"All right. Enough questions. The festival is about to start." Zandar held up a hand to stop Zeck's protest. "Mother will be back quick enough."

"Bye, Heko." Zeck looked up at Heko with a dejected expression.

Heko looked down at Zeck. "Bye, Zeck."

Heko followed Zandar out of the side gate into a wide street. Zandar grinned as they joined the stream of people flowing by. Heko bit back her own grin at Zandar's happiness to do something as simple as stepping outside her door and going to a festival.

"Thank you for answering Zeck's questions," Zandar said. "He's at that age where he wants to know about everything."

"No problem," Heko said. "I . . . uh . . . I've never talked to a little boy before."

Zandar stopped walking and stared at her in surprise. "What? Really?"

Heko stopped and turned to her. "Really."

Zandar walked at a more leisurely pace. "Was it strange?"

Heko pondered the question. "Yeah. It was, at first."

"How old were you when you saw your first male?" Zandar asked.

"Sixteen. When I came here," Heko said.

Zandar gave her another astonished look. "You mean that was the first time you ever left Emoria?"

"Sometimes we ventured to the bluffs overlooking Rihnon, just to look at the city," Heko said. "But we were too far away to distinguish the people from each other."

"I would love a chance to see Emoria one day." Zandar flashed her a dazzling smile, and then gazed ahead at the crowd gathering on the expanse of green in the middle of Balderon.

Heko opened her mouth, then closed it and fought every desire to blurt out her wish for Zandar to see Emoria, too. She realized Zandar didn't know such a statement from an Emoran warrior was a bold admission of interest. In Balderon, it was little more than polite conversation. Certain words and statements didn't seem to have as strong a weight to them as in Emoria.

"As a scholar studying Emoran warriors, I'm sure you'd be allowed to visit." She pretended to look at a group of colorfully dressed dancers to hide the rise of color in her cheeks.

Zandar gave her a curious look. "Perhaps if one of those warriors put in a good word for me."

Heko rapidly lost her boldness and nodded as she stared at her boots.

A thoughtful look flickered across Zandar's face, and then she smiled. "Everyone I know has been going to the festival since they were able to walk. It'll be fun sharing it with a visitor from out of town."

"Is that considered proper?" Heko frowned. "I mean I'm here as your guard."

Zandar seemed to dismiss the thought with a wave of her hand. "I would have been just as happy if you were dressed in ordinary Emoran clothes. But since I can't be here without a guard, you have to dress that way." She almost laughed at Heko's dumbfounded expression. "It's much nicer to have someone to talk."

Heko let out the breath she held. "So . . . uh . . ."

Zandar flashed an amused look. "Am I able to come to the festival with just a friendly companion? Only if I wanted to give my mother more headaches than she already has over my—in her words—total disregard for the way things should be done. But, truthfully, there are a lot of people who aren't quite as socially conscious as my mother, and who are here with friends just having a good time."

Heko nodded. "It's like that in Emoria. Only the bracer of flowers indicates more than friendship."

Zandar gave her a sidelong look. "Have you ever worn a bracer of flowers to the Festival of Flowers?"

Heko knew her cheeks were a deep red and wished Zandar didn't look so delighted about it. "We, uh, only wear bracers with the woman we want as our life companion."

"I guess you might be a bit young for such an important decision," Zandar said.

"I was when I left Emoria," Heko said.

"Which was . . ."

"Last summer." Heko followed Zandar into a maze of stalls of festival trinkets and just about every kind of ware she had ever seen. Smoke and aromas floated up from stalls of cooking meats and the fried balls of grains, spices, and vegetables that were popular in Balderon.

"So sixteen is a little young and seventeen is . . ."

"The age when Emorans begin to show serious interest," Heko said.

Zandar held up two fingers to a tea vendor. "So you decided to escape to Balderon?"

Heko chuckled. "Yeah. Something like that."

"The women in Emoria are that ugly?" Zandar gave the vendor a coin, took two mugs of spiced tea, and gave one to Heko.

Heko looked at her boots. "Too forward."

Zandar laughed. "How you warriors must suffer in Emoria. Until you find your life companion that is." She took a sip of her tea and looked around. "Are they Emorans?"

Heko took in Zandar's wide-eyed stare and turned around. She sighed in resignation. "Yes."

"Forget what I said about preferring you to walk around in everyday Emoran clothes. That would be way too much attention in my direction." Zandar cocked her head at Heko. "Are they going to tease you without mercy for merely talking to me?"

Heko tried to relax and keep within the spirit of Zandar's friendly banter. It was just friendly banter. Zandar didn't know that teasing alone was enough in Emoria to let a warrior know she was having serious thoughts about the warrior. Most women were merciful enough to give the warrior hints, so they weren't too stunned when they made the bold first move. "Oh, yeah."

"They're coming this way," Zandar said under her breath.

Heko crossed her arms as Taine and Nohi strolled up to them. "Zandar, I'd like you to meet my cousin, Nohi, and my best friend, Taine."

"Well met, Nohi. Well met, Taine," Zandar said.

Taine grinned. "Well met, Zandar."

Nohi bowed her head. "Well met, Zandar."

"Now that we have the formalities out of the way, you have to explain your braids to me." Zandar pointed at their belts. "Are you both warriors?"

"I'm a scout, and this is the scout's braid." Taine lifted a braid with green threads woven in the leather.

"And I'm an unbraided warrior," Nohi said. "That means I've done all the training to be a warrior but I haven't gone to Emoria to go through the initiation to earn the braid."

"So you're not from Emoria?" Zandar asked.

"I'm from Balderon," Nohi said.

"So what is your braid for?" Zandar asked.

"This braid means I've reached legal age," Nohi said.

"If you've lived here all your life, why didn't you tell your cousin about the Games? She looks like she could do well in several of the events." Zandar looked Heko up and down with an impish grin.

Nohi nodded. "She can handle herself pretty well in competition. The problem is, we promised her mothers we wouldn't let her get into any situation that might break that cute nose of hers."

Heko hid her embarrassment in her mug of tea.

Zandar pretended to consider the idea. "I would think a broken nose would give her a more menacing look."

Nohi shrugged. "You know mothers."

"I know mothers all right," Zandar said. "They have unreasonable ideas of what their daughters should be."

Heko gave Zandar a curious look, and then caught Taine's raised eyebrow that said she approved.

Zandar finished her tea and put the mug on the tea stall next to Heko's mug. "You don't mind if I ask all kinds of questions, do you? I just get so curious about things that I don't even know I'm doing it."

"No problem," Taine said. "As long as we can ask questions in return."

"A kind of fun cultural exchange." Zandar grinned in delight. "I can already tell this is going to be the best festival yet."

"Heko has told us of how members of merchants' families have to be careful in public," Taine said.

"I wish I had lived before the war." Zandar sighed. "I hate not having the same freedom as other people."

"You're in luck, then," Nohi said. "No one bothers Emorans. You can be at your ease with us around."

"I like that idea." Zandar's happy smile was so infectious, Heko struggled not to smile herself.

They spent the rest of the morning, strolling around the festival and chatting about the differences in customs and traditions. Heko was relieved she could just be with Zandar and not be the sole focus of her attention.

"Have you ever eaten at The Silver Goblet?" Zandar asked as they passed a sizable stone building on the edge of the green. Tables and benches crowded a stone courtyard, and the establishment overflowed with patrons. "It has the best tidbit platter in town and, best of all, my mother wouldn't be caught dead in such a—as she puts it—common place. Common meaning a place where all kinds of people patronize it simply because the food is good. Scandalous."

Her laugh was like sparkling music to Heko's ears.

"You should pay more attention to your mother," came a casual, hard-edged voice behind them.

They spun around.

Brandle sauntered up to them. Her show of colors was up-to-the-minute fashionable and almost painfully ostentatious. Heko tried to hide her disgust behind a bland expression.

Brandle glanced at the Emorans like they were little more than servants. "She may think you're taking your interest in military history a little too seriously, when you can't come home on time or even enjoy a day without finding common soldiers to research."

Zandar crossed her arms. "I haven't spoken to a common soldier all day."

Taine and Nohi looked impressed by Zandar's feistiness.

"What about your guard?" Brandle gave Heko an appraising once over.

"An Emoran warrior is anything but a common soldier," Zandar said.

"Emoran?" Brandle took another look at Heko, and then turned her attention to Taine and Nohi. "Still, I don't think your mother would be pleased you decided to see the festival with your guard's friends."

"I think she'd be pleased I'm surrounded by three well-trained Emoran warriors for the price of only one," Zandar said.

"No offense to Emoria," Brandle said, "but I've heard the reason they never join the Regulars is because their fighting skills are more boast than truth."

"The reason they don't join the Regulars is they don't want to spend six years away from Emoria," Zandar said. "The truth is always less sensational than rumor."

"Nonetheless, I think your mother would feel better if someone of your class accompanied you," Brandle gave the Emorans a mild look of disdain, "if you insist on keeping your current company. For appearances sake."

Zandar rubbed her chin. "It's nice that you're concerned, but

Emoria has no social distinctions, so my new friends and I are from the same class."

Brandle bristled with frustration and turned to Heko. "For the sake of Zandar's continual safety, since her mother has retained you to guard her to and from Artocia, I'd be interested in witnessing this legendary Emoran skill."

"Not that it's any of your business," Zandar said.

"Only because you haven't made it my business yet." Brandle returned her attention to Heko. "I've sponsored Kiki—a daughter of my household cook in the sword event. She's a soldier for the Southern Territories—the best trained force in the world."

"Sponsored?" Heko turned to Zandar.

"Everyone who participates in the Games has to have a sponsor willing to pay the entry fee," Zandar said.

Heko turned to Brandle. "I have to find a sponsor."

"You don't have to take this challenge, Heko," Zandar said. "She's just angry because I won't accept her festival token."

Brandle stiffened and glanced around. "You're too free with your tongue. Especially among strangers who don't understand our ways."

Zandar straightened and crossed her arms. "Heko is not a stranger. She's a friend. And my free tongue is never going to become any more imprisoned."

"Your mother—"

"My mother has never kept me or my tongue under lock and key," Zandar said. "This is your anger speaking."

Bramble tight jaw trembled as she struggled to keep control over her anger. "Are you afraid my soldier will beat your pet Emoran, and your mother will hire someone else to guard you?"

"Of course not." Zandar glanced at Heko.

Nohi put her hand on the hilt of her knife. "We will stand as guards while she enters the events, if that's why you hesitate."

Zandar turned to Brandle. "If Heko agrees to fight, I'll sponsor her."

Heko bowed her head. "I would be honored to represent you in the sword event." She caught Nohi and Taine's widening eyes at her boldness. At the beginning of a courtship, an Emoran warrior would never do more than a nod of agreement or a simple "I'll do it."

"And if I win?" Brandle said.

"I will not get caught up in any rash wagering," Zandar said. "This is only about your uncertainty about Heko's ability to protect me, if need be."

Fury and frustration flashed across Brandle's face. "Very well. The event is tomorrow morning. My soldier is favored to win the sword event, so you'd better let your pet warrior rest up and get some practice in today."

"I look forward to instructing your soldier in the way real warriors handle a sword," Heko said.

A hint of uncertainly flickered across Brandle's face, and Heko allowed a ghost of a feral grin.

# Chapter 11

"I'M GLAD YOU adjusted to how things are done here because my head is spinning." Taine plopped down at a table in the crowded common room of the safe house. Nohi squeezed in beside her, and Heko sat opposite them. "I can't believe she has no idea that only a woman who has already ensnared her warrior would tease and ask questions just to embarrass her."

"She doesn't know." Heko signaled for tea instead of ale and gratefully accepted the plate of stew.

Nohi rubbed her chin. "I'm not so sure about that."

Heko frowned at her. "She doesn't know."

"You said yourself she knows how women ensnare warriors," Nohi said.

"If she knew, she would know not to tease like she does," Heko said.

"But she knows that you're not acting the way you should be," Nohi said.

Heko blinked at her and put down a forkful of potatoes. "You told me to adapt to the way they do things here."

Nohi put down her fork and put her hands on her hips. "I can't help it you fell for a military historian with a special interest in warrior societies."

Heko sighed and munched on the potatoes. "So, are you saying we're kind of making it up as we go along?"

Nohi grinned. "Yeah, I guess I am."

Heko took a few moments to think that through. "But she still knows she has to make the first move."

Taine sat back and grinned. "I thought you didn't think she liked you like that."

Heko swallowed a sip of tea. "You, uh, spent the day with her. What do you think?"

"Ah, Balderon rules at the table." Nohi turned to Taine. "We took such pity on her from Zandar's teasing, we've forgotten to tease her ourselves."

Taine cocked her head at Heko. "I think she really likes you. She gives you these looks every once in a while. I can't even explain them—"

"She looks at you like she wants to get to know you better." Nohi grinned at Heko's unamused expression.

"Let's put it this way," Taine said. "If she didn't find you interesting, would she bother to tease you and try to embarrass you? She knows our traditions enough to know how you would be taking those actions."

"What about Brandle?" Heko glumly signaled for more tea.

"Zandar definitely doesn't like her," Taine said.

"Brandle thinks she and Zandar are going to be joined," Heko said. "And I don't think she's going to care if Zandar is forced into the joining or not. She's not about love. She's not about loyalty. She's certainly not about honor. She's about conquest."

"And all her mother cares about is a merger of their houses." Nohi gave Heko a speculative look. "If it came down to it, are you willing to add princess in front of your name to sway Zandar's mother?"

Heko knew her answer but searched for the proper words to explain it. "As much as I would want to do that, I won't play the same games as Brandle and treat Zandar like some kind of object rather than a woman with a free will. I'll only do it if Zandar makes the first move, and we have an understanding before she knows who I am."

Taine leaned forward on her elbows. "But what if Brandle and Zandar's mother settles the terms of joining before Zandar has a chance to let you know she's interested?"

Heko stared down at her mug of tea.

"Look, Heko," Nohi said. "Life is full of taking chances. And one of the biggest chances we take is when we hope someone feels the same way about us as we feel about them. My gut tells me your being a princess wouldn't make any difference to Zandar."

"But I'd never really know for sure," Heko said.

Taine shook her head. "Do you doubt Niko's love for Hyek?"

Heko looked up, shocked and indignant. "Of course not."

"But Niko knew Hyek was a princess," Taine said.

"Would Laur have allowed them to be joined or gifted them with a child if their love wasn't true?" Nohi asked.

"But . . . but everyone didn't stare at Hyek all the time." Heko was confused and miserable.

"I know I never thought I'd ever hear myself saying this," Taine said, "but Zandar is attracted to your brains. I don't think what you look like makes a bit of difference to her."

"Not only your brains, but she likes your personality," Nohi said.

Heko stared at them as if their ale had gone to their heads. "Brains? Personality? Compared to her I don't have either."

Taine and Nohi chuckled.

Heko gave them a baffled look. "What's so funny?"

"You certainly can hold your own with a University student," Nohi said.

"Huh?"

"I could keep up with only a part of that discussion on the battle of Leiker you had with her," Taine said.

"You're not a warrior," Heko said.

"When you started counting the number of paces the Southern Territories soldiers took on the bridge to be exactly in range to strike the Liekerians down with arrows, I was in awe in how you could envision that," Nohi said.

"But she's a lot smarter than I am." Heko rubbed her forehead with her fingers. How could she explain how much she didn't know? "She's study so many different subjects and reads all the time."

"She may know more than you do, but that doesn't make her any smarter," Nohi said. "You understood her, and were able to follow her ideas, once you got all the facts. That's being intelligent."

Heko bit her lip and tried to incorporate the idea into her ever expanding view of the world. "I'll have to think about it."


HEKO WAS A little nervous about wearing her Emoran leathers, but Zandar had insisted she properly represent herself for the competition. It didn't help that Taine and Nohi were waiting to see Zandar's reaction to her in all her Emoran warrior glory.

A side door slammed open, and Zeck bounded into the courtyard and stopped as if he hit an invisible wall. He stared in awe at Heko.

"Zeck, slow down, the competition isn't going anywhere." Ponadin's voice held a light good humor Heko had never heard before from her.

Ponadin and Zandar came out of the side door.

"Ah, Heko." Ponadin smiled. "I was so delighted to hear that Zandar is going to sponsor you in the sword competition." She gave

Heko an appraising look. "Yes, I think you could beat Brandle's pet soldier. It hasn't been any fun the last few years because no one has been able to put up someone capable of beating her." She took in Taine and Nohi. "And are these your friends who have volunteered to guard Zandar while you're helping me win a friendly wager with Brandle?"

"Yes, ma'am," Heko said.

Ponadin put a small hat on her head. "If we had more Emorans as guards, those thieves would have fled a long time ago. Come along, Zeck."

Zeck broke away from his spell and trotted after Ponadin to the waiting coach.

Heko had barely heard Ponadin's words. She was concentrating on keeping a blush from her cheeks as Zandar gazed at her with an expression far worse than the awestruck stares she usually received. Zandar's expression was a different kind of stunned. A deeper, introspective stunned that Zandar slowly blinked out of and replaced with a pleasantly puzzled expression by the time her mother and Zeck climbed into their coach.

Nohi and Taine exchanged amused looks.

"I thought your mother wouldn't be too happy with you being guarded by a couple of strangers while your guard competed," Nohi said.

Heko gave her a grateful look for breaking a potentially awkward silence.

Zandar shook her head and grinned. "It made my mother's day. I finally demonstrated—in her mind—some of that merchant blood flowing through me. The Games are a big part of the social games merchants play. They sponsor competitors, engage in friendly wagering, give themselves false status, and a false sense of importance when their competitors win."

Nohi grinned. "Are you regretting this sudden show of conformity?"

Zandar looked at Heko, and the twinkle that had been subdued by whatever possessed her when she first entered the courtyard came back into her eyes. "I sponsored Heko because I knew Emoran warriors never back down from a challenge. And besides, I'd love to see someone finally cut some notches into Brandle's arrogant expectations that whatever she wants she gets."

Heko straightened. "It would be my pleasure to cut Brandle down as many notches as you desire."

Zandar gave her a thoughtful look. "Her manner must be very foreign to you."

Heko gritted her teeth and worked to keep her opinion to herself.

Zandar gave her a sad smile. "I think it's interesting she considers you little more than a servant. Yet you possess the polite manners and respect of other people's feelings the merchant class is supposed to possess, but only use when trying to get something we want from each other." She walked past the Emorans to the gate and looked back. "I'm glad you have the opportunity to teach us some manners."

Heko's jaw dropped open as she stared at her. Taine and Nohi looked equally stunned. Heko exchanged amazed glances with them as they followed Zandar through the gate.

They walked in an ever growing stream of people buzzing with excitement through the city to the east gate that opened onto Balderon Valley. Heko sent prayers to Laur that Zandar wouldn't notice all the heads turning as they went by. She held her breath when Zandar glanced around with a puzzled expression.

Zandar turned to Heko. "Is everyone staring at you?"

Taine and Nohi sputtered out a laugh.

"It's a problem Heko has," Taine said. "People were staring at her all day yesterday but the Emoran leathers cause a more obvious reaction."

Zandar frowned. "I thought they were just looking at her because she's one of the more popular guards and is a familiar face in Balderon."

Heko sighed and tried to slump.

"By the end of the day, they'll be staring at you because you'll have beaten the soldier who's won the sword competition five years in a row." Zandar slapped Heko on the back and strode through the gate.

Taine and Nohi stared after her in astonishment.

"Wow. She's brave," Taine muttered.

Heko shrugged.

They went through the city gate in a surging crowd and stopped and stared in amazement.

Heko drank in the tents, the pavilions, and the small arena that must have taken a good while to construct. The sounds of clashing swords reached her ears, and a joy that inhabited her soul sprang forth.

"I love the Games." Zandar put out her arms and pretended to breathe in the excitement-charged air.

They all laughed, and Zandar led the way around crowded tents of vendors' stalls and pavilions with banners for each Game event fluttering outside them. Heko studied the warriors gathered around these pavilions. Warriors with nothing better to do than guard cities and participate in games.

They approached the pavilion closest to the arena. The fluttering banner had an ornate image of a sword on it.

"There are only four events in the games so everyone can see all of them," Zandar said. "We're going to get Heko signed in, and then go watch the staff competition."

They stepped into the airy pavilion with a canopy fluttering far overhead. Heko reveled in the aroma of oiled steel and leather and the sounds of blades slipping out of scabbards for inspection.

"You're not competing are you?" Sarie walked up to Heko.

Heko shrugged. "I got challenged."

Sarie shook her head. "Someone's got to teach you your idea of a challenge isn't the same as ours."

"Brandle didn't think I could beat her soldier," Heko said.

Sarie whistled, and several soldiers exchanged glances. "That's what I call a challenge. Tell you what. We'll forgive you for competing this year if you beat Kiki. And if you promise never to compete again."

Heko blinked at Sarie. "I need to ask my sponsor."

The soldiers turned to Zandar with expectant expressions.

Zandar gave Heko a sidelong look. "You must be pretty good." She turned to the soldiers, who watched her with pleading eyes. "My purpose for sponsoring Heko is so she can respond to the challenge made to her honor as a warrior, so if she wishes to agree to your request then it's all right with me."

Heko gave a decisive nod. "Then I agree. If I win, I promise I won't compete in the sword competition again."

The soldiers exchanged glances.

"Since we've never seen how you handle other weapons, we agree," Sarie said.

Taine and Nohi chuckled.

"Anything is a formidable weapon in Heko's hands," Taine said.

Sarie crossed her arms. "I still don't understand why Emoria is letting one of their best warriors live in Balderon playing smith and shopkeeper and auxiliary guard."

Heko shrugged. "Expanding one's knowledge and skill beyond warrioring is considered a good thing to do."

"I like the theory that you couldn't turn around without bumping into a love-struck girl much better," Sarie said.

"The burden of being too cute to be a warrior," Radle said.

The other soldiers laughed and nudged each other.

Heko wished she could rub away the pink she knew colored her cheeks, and was grateful it was her turn to sign in.

Zandar stepped up to a small table. A woman who wore an official sash looked up expectantly.

"I wish to sponsor Heko . . ." Zandar turned to Heko.

"Ketlas," Heko said.

"Heko Ketlas," Zandar said.

The woman squinted up at Heko. She looked as if she had seen her share of battles in the last war. "Age?"

"Seventeen," Heko said.

"Training?"

"I have my warrior braid." Heko lifted the end of the braid with her fingers.

The woman half-stood and leaned over the table. She gazed at the braid with interest. "We've never had an Emoran in the competition and have never seen an Emoran fight, so we have no point of comparison for your skill." She sat back down. "No contestant can be below the skill level of a fully-trained soldier."

"I believe there are several soldiers of Balderon who are familiar with Heko's skill." Zandar turned around. They had attracted a curious audience.

Sarie and Radle stepped forward.

"We've fought with her," Sarie said. "She's the best warrior I've ever seen."

"According to the other Emorans, she's the best warrior in Emoria," Radle said.

Heko frowned and wondered what other wild exaggerations were being spread about her.

"You fought with swords?" the woman asked.

"Yes," Sarie and Radle said.

The woman returned her attention to Heko. "Let's see your sword."

Heko unsheathed her sword and handed it to the woman.

"Nice." The woman stood and whipped it around. "This is a master weapon."

"Emorans are always issued the best blades we make," Heko said.

The woman stared at her in astonishment. "This is regular issue in Emoria?"

Heko looked at Nohi and Taine, who unsheathed their swords. The surrounding soldiers muttered their appreciation.

My mother made this sword and Heko's," Nohi said.

"Impressive." The woman nodded and returned Heko's sword to her. "Three pieces of silver, and both of you have to sign this document of registration."

Zandar gave the coins to the woman and signed the document. Heko put her signature next to Zandar's.

"Beating soldiers of Balderon is not the same as beating a soldier of the Southern Territories." Brandle's voice came from behind them.

They spun around. A large woman with bulky muscles and a sour demeanor stood next to a smug Brandle.

Heko straightened. "If that's your soldier, then it'll be the same."

Kiki's face hardened, and she lunged forward. A half-dozen soldiers from Balderon grabbed her.

"You won't have a chance to find out because you're not going to make it past the first round," she said.

"What if you're my opponent in the first round?" Heko asked.

"As returning champion I don't have to fight until the third round," Kiki said.

"Then I'll have a nice warm-up before I teach you how to use that sword." Heko nodded at the hilt peeking over Kiki's shoulder.

"And I'll be watching you get beat before you have a chance to lift your sword in the first round," Kiki said. "My only regret is I won't be teaching you what a real soldier is made of myself."

"You won't have to worry about missing a chance to fight me," Heko said. "If you knock yourself out with your own sword before you face me in competition, you've still insulted me, and that equals a challenge in Emoria. You'll get your fight one way or another."

Kiki looked her up and down in disdain. "I look forward to it."

"Now this is what the Games are all about," Brandle said with a smug smile. "Something to make it fun for all of us. Come on, Kiki. Let's get you signed in."

Zandar led the Emorans out of the pavilion and dramatically blew out a breath. She turned to Heko. "For someone who's quiet and unassuming, you certainly know how to get everyone's attention."

Heko shrugged and gave her a sheepish grin.

# Chapter 12

HEKO STEPPED INTO the oblong arena and gazed up at the towering rows of spectators. Many more people crowded the seats and standing areas than there had been for the staff competition. They stomped and chanted so loud that Heko's ears popped.

The crowd suddenly quieted and Heko turned around. Her opponent strolled on the hard packed dirt from the other side of the area.

The other warrior looked competent enough—a soldier of the Southern Territories. Tall, strong, with a confident gaze as she sized up Heko. She kept glancing at Kiki, who stood in one of the warm-up pits.

Kiki was giving her rather animated signals with her hands. Interesting. Heko hid her amusement as she looked at the sidelines. Zandar was watching her with intense anticipation. She gave Heko a wave and a nod of encouragement. Heko nodded back. A giddiness rose up inside her from just seeing Zandar.

A grizzled warrior walked to the middle of the arena. "The next competitors are Isab Trede of the Southern Territories Regulars and Heko Ketlas of Emoria."

The crowd murmured. They all seemed to be straining to get a look at Heko. She ignored them and faced her competitor.

"The first warrior to get three touches of aggression wins." The warrior looked at Isab and then Heko and strode to the sidelines.

Heko and Isab circled each other, making a show of sizing the other up.

Isab unsheathed her sword. Zandar had explained this was supposed to be an action of intimidation. Heko still couldn't shake her lifelong belief that it was a sign of cowardice. Isab casually showed off her ability to flip her sword. Heko stopped circling and crossed her arms.

"This is a sword competition, not a staring contest," Isab said.

Heko shook out her arms. "So, stop staring and come at me."

The crowd hushed and went so still, Heko could hear the banners at the top of the arena flapping.

Isab looked uncertain for a moment then backed away to prepare her first move. She swiped low and caught air. Heko sidestepped around her and tapped her on the shoulder. Isab spun her blade around. Heko flipped over Isab and backed away several paces. Isab turned around.

Heko reached over her shoulder and unsheathed her sword. Isab lunge forward and crashed her sword against Heko's in several thrusts and parries. Heko could feel Isab going all out and was impressed by her skill.

Isab bounced back and flipped her sword as if waiting for Heko to be the aggressor. She lifted her sword and ran at Heko.

Heko put her blade out and stopped Isab's blade. She slid her blade until the swords were hilt to hilt and then gave it a delicate twist and shoved Isab away.

"First touch," Heko said.

"What?" Isab reacted and then looked at her finger. A sliver of blood ran down it.

The old warrior approached them and inspected the small wound. "First touch." She trotted to the sidelines.

"You got lucky," Isab said. "But you can't win on festival tricks. I don't think you have it in you to attack."

Heko rested her blade on her shoulder. "Emorans don't like to attack fighters with lesser skill than themselves."

The arena went still as death.

Isab narrowed her eyes at Heko. "You've never seen me fight before, yet you refused to draw your sword before I made the first move."

"I didn't need to see you fight." Heko casually flipped her sword. "I could tell your skill by the way you walked into the arena, by the way you circled and sized me up, by the way you unsheathed your sword. Your body is the temple upon which your skill rests, and if it is imperfect in balance and movement without your sword, it will be imperfect with it."

Isab frowned and then straightened. "I think you're just covering your fear of attacking with nonsense."

Heko tossed her sword in the air and flipped up to catch it. She landed in a roll that brought her a sword's length from Isab. She pointed her sword, forcing Isab into a defensive position, and avoided

Isab's attempt to parry with efficient, subtle moves. She flicked at Isab's arm and then at the other. She stepped back.

"Two touches," Heko said.

"What?" Isab, fuming with indignation, glared at the rips in the leather on her arms and the growing stains.

Heko sheathed her sword and crossed her arms. "I attacked. Isn't that what you wanted?"

The crowd erupted in laughter and applause and the tension flowed out of the arena.

The old warrior approached them and inspected Isab's wounds. "Two touches. The bout goes to Heko Ketlas of Emoria."

The crowd jumped to their feet and cheered. Heko blinked up at them in surprised as she walked to the sidelines. Her heart faltered at the sight of Zandar bouncing up and down with excitement.

"Bal's Children," Zandar said, breathless. "I've seen Isab fight, she's one of the best. And she looked like a novice next to you. How did Emorans gain such a great understanding of the art of fighting?"

"It's in our blood," Heko said as she brushed off her leathers.

"She's being modest," Nohi said. "We start with learning how not to fight. To focus on everything that happens around us that has nothing to do with using the weapon. Focusing on using the weapon closes off other important stimuli, but focusing on everything else, the weapon becomes a part of that environment—harmonious with it."

"So you have to forget that it's a sharp, very dangerous thing," Zandar said.

Nohi nodded. "That's exactly it. These soldiers are taught to fear their weapons and are taught ways to keep themselves safe from the blade while trying to inflict wounds on others. We are never taught to fear the sword but to make it a part of our soul."

Isab put a hand on Nohi's arm. "What do you mean?"

They turned to Isab. She looked both angry and confused.

"So you're saying it's just a different approach to training?" she asked.

Heko grasped her shoulder. "You're a good fighter. Excellent technique. The best I've seen since I left Emoria."

Isab stared at her, looking even more confused. "How could you tell? I barely had a chance to fight. And what about all those jibes?"

The clash of swords rang through the arena as the next pair of opponents started their bout. The crowd roared with appreciation.

"I can tell from the way you carry your body, the confidence you have with your sword, and the power of your hits," Heko said. "I did not jibe, I spoke the truth."

Isab opened her mouth, closed it, and opened it again. Then she sighed. "You did speak the truth."

"I noticed your friend Kiki was trying to give you pointers on how to fight me." Heko nodded at the warm-up pit. "You're a better fighter than she is, yet she's the champion of this competition."

"Have you ever seen her fight?" Isab asked.

"No." Heko grinned. "But I've seen her move. She has too many overdeveloped, nonfunctional muscles to handle the sword with more than a brute competency."

Zandar stared astonished at Heko.

Taine laughed. "She's a genius about anything that has to do with warrioring."

"Then how come none of us seem to be able to beat her?" Isab asked.

"Because she uses the muscles and her arrogance to intimidate," Heko said. "Everything about her is intended to intimidate so she doesn't have to use any real skill."

Isab rubbed her chin in thought. "I've never lost in the first round before. In fact, the last three years, I fought Kiki for the festival sash." She crossed her arms. "I want to learn more about your approach to fighting."

"Visit with the Emorans in Ynit," Heko said.

"They can fight like this?"

"The ones trained as warriors can," Heko said.

Isab gave her an amused look. "I can imagine their reaction to a soldier sauntering into the safe house and asking to learn your training technique. Can I mention that you sent me?"

"Uh . . ."

"Tell them Nohi Leatas sent you," Nohi said. "They know me there, and Heko's too fresh out of Emoria for them to know her."

Heko caught Zandar's frown and prayed she accepted Nohi's story.

"I'll do that." Isab nodded. "I was angry for being beaten in such a way, but now I see it as an opportunity to become a better warrior. I thank you for the lesson." She bowed her head and, instead of going back to Kiki, who was staring at her with increasing curiosity and impatience from the other side of the arena, she went to a group of Regulars who were watching the current bout.

"Let's go sit in my mother's box until you have to fight again." Zandar led them to outside the arena.

Heko sucked in a breath of fresh air. The atmosphere inside the arena was suffocating and charged with too high of energy for her liking.

The outside of the arena had several sets of steps that snaked up the sides to landings on each tier lined with arched openings. They climbed to the uppermost tier and through an opening to a narrow corridor that followed the outer wall.

Zandar walked them past several small doors, each painted with the colors of a different merchant house. She stopped in front of the door striped with gold and black for the House of Ponadin and gently knocked.

The door opened.

"Do you have room for four more?" Zandar asked.

"Of course. Come in." Ponadin rose from her seat on the edge of a balcony and motioned them in. "Let me see your talented champion."

Rewner stood from his seat next to Ponadin, and Zandar guided Heko to it.

"Now I see why thieves leave Emorans alone." Ponadin clasped her hands together in delight as she sat down.

Heko sank onto the seat and looked back at Taine and Nohi. They sat next to Rewner, and Zandar squeezed into the seat between Heko and the side of the balcony.

"Brandle refused to wager until after she saw you, and now she won't make a wager at all." Ponadin sighed. "She's down there filling Kiki's ears with instructions. That kind of tenaciousness makes her the great merchant she is." She glanced at Zandar, but Zandar had both elbows on the balcony as she watched the competition far below.

Heko swallowed the realization that no matter how well Ponadin treated her, she didn't see her as anything more than a guard for hire. That Ponadin didn't think someone skilled enough to make a soldier from Ynit look like a novice was someone who would be interested in her daughter or . . . who may have caught her daughter's interest.

She turned to watch the pair of fighters and found Zandar, still leaning on the balcony, gazing at her with thoughtful eyes. She was too startled to look away, and their eyes locked for several heartbeats.

The crowd roared, and they blinked, then looked down to watch the competition.

Heko couldn't breathe. She had never experienced a blow in a fight as disabling as the blow from looking in Zandar's eyes. She ached to gaze into those eyes again, to hold her hand, to kiss her . . . She sucked in her breath. She was a goner.


HEKO HAD SEEN enough of Kiki's arrogant attitude in the early rounds to know she didn't want to put up with that attitude when she faced her. She took her place at the edge of the fighting pit.

Zandar put a hand on Heko's arm. "Good luck."

Heko grinned at her. "Thank you for sponsoring me."

Zandar grinned back. "I knew you'd have fun."

They watched as Kiki sauntered up to her place on the opposite side, her arrogant bravado in place.

"This will be fun," Heko said.

"For the festival sash," the old warrior announced from the center of the arena, "we have the defending champion Kiki Jette, of the Southern Territories Regulars, and Heko Ketlas, warrior of Emoria."

The overflowing crowd popped Heko's ears with their roar of anticipation as the old warrior walked out of the fighting pit.

Kiki bounded into the middle of the arena and unsheathed her sword. "Come on, you trickster. That's what they call you in Emoria, isn't it? I dare you to face me without a flip or a roll or any other acrobatics."

Heko strolled into the fighting pit and stopped a few paces from Kiki. "All right."

Kiki narrowed her eyes. "Then prepare to learn from a master."

She swung her sword around her head and ran forward.

Heko ducked, shot her hand out, and poked Kiki in the wrist. She backed off as the sword landed in the soft dirt.

Kiki slid to a stop, turned around, and stared at her sword.

"You're not going to call that a festival trick are you?" Heko asked. "Because where I come from, that's the first move we learn when we begin sword training."

Kiki picked up her sword and kept her confident arrogance in place. "You Emorans can spin whatever stories you want, since none of us really know how you're trained."

"We spend the first year of our training without ever touching a sword or any weapon." Heko shook out her arms. "We're taught first to fight with our bodies—to face weaponed opponents with nothing but the speed and the skill to stop them. In doing that we never learn the fear of weapons. We turn our bodies into weapons first, and when we finally have a sword or staff or bow in our hands, they simply become extensions of our primary weapon—our bodies."

"It doesn't matter what kind of fanciful story you weave. To win this competition you have to make your touches of aggression with a sword." Kiki lunged forward. Heko ducked. Kiki rolled over her, and Heko grabbed the back of Kiki's sword hand and shaved off a patch of leather on Kiki's leg with the blade.

Heko straightened and back away. "The rules don't say whose sword has to be used."

Kiki climbed to her feet and stared at her leg—blood seeped from a thin neat line. Her shocked expression was quickly replaced by outrage as the old warrior trotted to her and inspected the wound.

Kiki jerked her leg away. "You're not going to let her get away with that are you?"

The old warrior straightened and leveled a gaze at her. "The rules only say that the wound must be caused by a sword blade."

"But this is the sword competition," Kiki said. "The crowd wants to see swords in combat."

The crowd remained still and expectant.

Kiki looked around in disbelief. "I can't believe you find this a satisfactory entertainment."

Heko pulled her sword from its sheath, the hiss cutting through the silence. "Are you saying you haven't found the bout entertaining enough?" She flipped her sword, and the old warrior scampered to the sidelines. "You want me to fight you with a sword?" She took a step forward. "You'd better think real hard before you answer, because I'll show no mercy."

The crowd sucked in a collective breath, and all eyes were riveted on Kiki.

Kiki flipped her blade and circled Heko who turned to follow her path. "I also won't show any mercy."

They circled for too long.

"It's against the Emoran warrior oath to make the first move of aggression against someone who is not Emoran," Heko said. "If you don't want to be here all day, you'll have to make the first move. If you dare, that is."

"Another fancy thing you could have just made up," Kiki said.

"So, are you afraid to attack?" Heko stopped circling and laid her blade on her shoulder.

Kiki straightened. "I'm not afraid of anything, much less you."

"I don't see you attacking." Heko looked up at the crowd. "Are you afraid the spectators will be disappointed when the bout is over within ten heartbeats after you attack?"

Kiki stared at Heko. "You'll be too busy fighting off my attack to get any more nicks in."

"I'm sure the spectators will keep the count for us," Heko said.

Kiki gave Heko another long stare. "No ducking."

Heko nodded. "No ducking."

Kiki flipped her sword around in patterns of eight, a move meant to hide where the strike would finally come from. Heko stood, looking unimpressed, with the blade still resting on her shoulder. Kiki whipped past Heko for a sideswipe, and the crowd started to count. Heko bounced away from the sword, and as Kiki found only air and stumbled, Heko hopped back and etched matching patterns in the leather covering Kiki's shoulder blades.

The word "five" echoed in the arena as the spectators stopped its count and waited in breathless silence.

Kiki spun around and ran toward Heko. Heko put up her sword and stopped Kiki's blade. The bout was over, and, as far as Heko was concerned, the challenge fight was just starting. She whipped her sword around and hooked Kiki's sword and sent it to flying into the soft dirt. She tripped Kiki onto her back and put the tip of her sword against Kiki's throat.

Kiki struggled and watched Heko with wide eyes.

Heko looked up at the spectators. "I only competed in this competition because I was challenged, and Emoran warriors never refuse a challenge. Let it be witnessed that I have won that challenge by pinning Kiki in a position she can only escape by either dying or me releasing her." The crowd murmured. "I also promised the soldiers of Balderon that if I beat Kiki, I would never compete in the sword competition again."

The spectators twittered in disappointment.

Heko stepped away from Kiki and sheathed her sword.

Kiki scrambled to her feet and felt her throat and looked at her fingers. No blood. The old warrior approached her and inspected the wounds on her shoulder blades.

The old warrior raised her eyes to the spectators. "Two touches. The festival sash goes to Heko Ketlas of Emoria."

The spectators jumped to their feet and roared their appreciation.

Heko turned to the sidelines and saw the only prize she desired from the competition—Zandar's dazzling smile.

"I still think you're nothing but a trickster," Kiki said, pulling Heko's attention away from Zandar. "We will fight again."

"Look forward to it. Bring some friends," Heko said over her shoulder as the old warrior led her to the podium where the mayor of Balderon waited with the sash. She'd endure a thousand ceremonies just for the opportunity to have Zandar smile at her.

# Chapter 13

HEKO COULDN'T KEEP away her grin. She was glad it was after dusk, and no one she knew was around to witness it. The last day of the festival had been magical. Something—unspoken and intangible but definitely real—had changed between her and Zandar. Something that left her giddy inside and in a constant state of wonderment. Even two days later, the feeling remained strong within her.

She turned the corner onto the wide boulevard with stately trees on isles of green down the middle of it. Ponadin's invitation for an after evening meal visit—a social activity among the upper classes of Balderon—came as a surprise. She'll probably be treated like a pet warrior, but the visit would be worth it if she got to see Zandar.

Something stung her neck and then clattered to the cobblestone. She spun around at the sound of a half-dozen ruffians running at her from the corner. Her mind told her to prepare to defend herself even as her body crashed to the ground.


"A FALL JOINING is good." Taine lifted a long narrow crate off the back of a wagon. "We could spend the winter in Emoria."

She carried the crate through the forge and into the back room of the blades shop.

"I suppose I'll have to get my braid if I want to make myself useful as a warrior." Nohi followed Taine with another crate.

Taine grinned. "I think that would be a good idea."

"Taine. Nohi." Lise ran into the shop from the little door that connected to the safe house. "Heko's been hurt."

"Hurt?" Taine grabbed Lise's arm.

"The boy on the coach said she was beaten up," Lise said.

"Coach." Nohi headed for the door followed by Taine and Lise.

Taine almost froze with fear when she saw an anxious-looking Haren next to the coach, surrounded by an ever growing crowd of Emorans pouring out of the safe house.

Haren rushed to them. "Heko was houses away from the House of Ponadin when it happened."

"What happened?" Nara pushed through the Emorans.

"I saw it all. I was at the front gate to let her in," Haren said. "She was walking along, and suddenly she stopped. She tried to turn around but crumpled to the ground. We found a dart—the healer has it. Anyway, a group of ruffians came around the corner and started kicking and hitting her with clubs and sticks. Within heartbeats several people were running to her rescue, and the ruffians ran off."

"Did they get caught?" Nara asked.

"They got one of them," Haren said.

Nara nodded and turned to Nohi and Taine. "You two go see Heko, and I'll see what I can find out about her attackers."

Nohi put a hand on Nara's arm. "Don't send a message to her mothers . . . yet. Heko's not ready to return to Emoria."

Nara gave Nohi and Taine a long look. "I'll discuss it with Heko first."

"Thank you," Nohi said. "You're the best."

Nara waved her hands. "Now go and send word back as soon as you can."

Nohi and Taine went to the coach. Haren held the door open for them, and they climbed in.

Taine looked around the interior in surprise as they settled on opposite seats.

"This is what Heko's been traveling in?" Taine fingered the soft material and bounced on the cushioned seat.

"Being a guard is a tough job," Nohi said.

Taine sat back as the coach lurched and rattled on the cobblestone. "Being Heko is the tough job. If she's not all right . . ."

"She's all right." Nohi bit her lip.

Taine sighed and stared out the window. "Whoever did it, knew how to bring her down."

"We know who did it." Nohi clenched her fists.

"We don't know for sure." Taine gazed at her. "We can't do anything until we know for sure."

"Will whoever did it be subjected to Emoran law?"

Taine shook her head. "She wasn't attacked in the safe house."

"So it doesn't matter that she's our princess?"

Taine shrugged. "Hyek could declare war on whoever did it, but I don't think that would accomplish much."

Nohi sighed and stared out the small window as they rattled into the upper class neighborhoods on the southern edge of the city.

The coach slowed down and stopped.

"Finally." Taine leaned out the window and saw a closed gate. "C'mon, c'mon."

She burst out of the coach, followed by Nohi, ready to climb the gate. A young woman inside the gate lifted the locking bars and pulled it open.

They ran up the long stone path to the front door, which opened as they approached. They clambered inside and slid to a stop on the polished flagstone floor and blinked up at the spacious multi-storied circular foyer.

"Taine, Nohi." Zandar stood up from a stone bench near a staircase that arched along the wall to the next floor.

"How is she?" Taine asked as they went to Zandar.

"Meners, the healer, is with her," Zandar said.

She led them through a maze of corridors lined with doors and opened ante-chambers, filled with an opulence Taine had never seen before. The sounds of the kitchen echoed from somewhere further into the wing. Zandar walked through an archway into what looked like a sitting room.

"We can wait here. She's in there." Zandar nodded at a closed door.

"Thanks," Nohi said as she and Taine settled on a low couch.

Zandar sat cross-legged in a chair. "Uh, will this mean that . . ." She studied her knee. "Does this mean that she'll have to go back to Emoria? I know she's not of legal age and everything . . ."

"My mother isn't going to say anything to her mothers until we know how she is and who did it," Nohi said. "Heko wouldn't be happy if Emoria found out about this incident before she had a chance to voice her desire to stay in Balderon."

"Do you think she'll want to stay after this?" Zandar asked.

Taine exchanged glances with Nohi. "She wants to stay."

"But what if she's, like, ordered to go home?" Zandar gazed down at her hands. "She must be a valuable warrior in Emoria."

"She came here right after she earned her braid," Taine said. "She left before taking on warrior duties. Besides, if she's ordered back, she'll defy that order."

Zandar's eyes widened. "Won't she get into trouble?"

Nohi and Taine chuckled.

"Not Heko," Taine said. "Emoria wants her to take as much time as she needs to satisfy her restless curiosity about the outside world, so when she returns to Emoria, she'll be ready to settle down."

"Because she's such a good warrior?" Zandar asked.

"Yeah." Taine studied the closed door. "She's the best."

Zandar put a hand on Taine's knee. "She'll be all right."

Taine looked up. "You know, I've known her since I was born, and we've been blood sisters since we were six. I've never seen her injured beyond a few bruises and scrapes, and those were usually from trying some silly stunt and not fighting. Her skill is in her speed."

"I've never seen anyone move so fast." Zandar straightened and brightened a bit. "One good thing. Her nose didn't get hit."

Nohi and Taine blinked at her and then chuckled.

"Her mothers will be happy to hear that," Nohi said.

The door opened, and a small white-haired woman entered the room. She looked surprised to see Taine and Nohi.

Zandar, Taine, and Nohi jumped to their feet.

"How is she?" Zandar asked. "Can we see her?"

Taine and Nohi exchanged glances at Zandar's strong concern.

"She got bruised up pretty good, some cuts and abrasions from whatever they used to hit her," Meners said. "No broken bones or internal injuries."

"What knocked her out?" Nohi asked.

"Nothing was on the dart and the wound was clean of any substance." Meners put her hands on the small of her back and stretched. "That leaves a penetration spell. Unfortunately, one with some rather unpleasant side effects."

Taine frowned. "A spell?"

"What kind of side effects?" Nohi asked.

"Fever, chills, coughing," Meners said. "Her lungs are affected to some extent. My recommendation is she not even think about leaving her bed until the spell wears off."

"Lungs?" Taine asked, panicked.

"Since it's a spell, she'll be fine when it wears off if she doesn't do anything to aggravate the symptoms," Meners said. "She's going to feel pretty miserable for a while. I left some herbs on the side table to make her more comfortable."

"Thank you, Meners," Zandar said. "My mother is waiting in the front parlor for you."

Meners bowed her head and walked out of the chamber.

Taine and Nohi stared at the door and hesitated.

Zandar gave them a puzzled look. "What's wrong?"

Taine rubbed her head and wandered around the room. "I've never seen Heko sick."

"The idea of seeing her so weak and injured . . ." Nohi put her head in her hands and stared at the floor.

"I think she wants to see you," Zandar said.

Taine took a deep breath and faced the opened doorway. She stepped into the chamber and stopped, confronted by a sitting room with a large fireplace. She looked past the cushioned chairs and low tables to a bed against the far wall.

"I can do this," she mumbled as she walked across the chamber, followed by Nohi and Zandar.

They stood next to the bed and stared down at Heko.

"Laur's waterfalls," Taine breathed.

Heko was curled up on her side, soaked in sweat, and looking beyond miserable. Her breaths came in labored rasps and her arms—the only part of her body besides her head not covered by a blanket—were purple with bruises. A bandage was wrapped around one hand and around an upper arm.

"We can't let my mother see her," Nohi said. "Not like this."

"How are we going to stop her?" Taine couldn't keep down her rising panic. "Any excuse will just make her suspicious."

"Don't let them take me home," Heko rasped in a weak whisper.

Taine knelt next to the bed. "Nara promised not to contact Emoria without talking to you first."

"Thank you," Heko breathed.

"Besides," Nohi stepped up next to Taine, "the healer said you're not supposed to leave this bed until the spell wears off."

"My mothers . . ." Heko coughed and grimaced from the pain. "My mothers will want me home."

"You worry about getting better and we'll make sure that you aren't taken to Emoria," Taine said.

"Can't leave yet," Heko mumbled and then sank into sleep.

"You'll have to figure out how to keep Heko here." Zandar gave them an almost panicked look. "My mother won't legally be able to go against family wishes."

"No one will move her until her lungs are all right." Taine settled down her racing thoughts. "Heko's just exhausted and in pain and is not thinking straight."

Zandar nodded and gazed down at Heko. "If this is my fault . . ."

Nohi and Taine exchanged startled looks.

"Your fault?" Nohi asked.

"If Brandle is behind this . . ."

Taine scratched her head. "Even if she is, why would it be your fault?"

Zandar tucked the blanket around Heko's exposed arm. "Because Brandle is trying to court me, and Heko got caught in the middle of it."

"And I thought the courtships in Emoria got rough," Taine said.

"What I mean is, Brandle's trying to court me, and I'm not interested." Zandar ran a hand through her hair, clearly frustrated. "Apparently, I'm the only person in Balderon who has ever said no to her, and she doesn't seem to know what the word means. So if Brandle had something to do with this, Heko got beat up because I refuse to breathe the same air as Brandle."

"If it's true, don't beat yourself up about it." Nohi put a hand on Zandar's shoulder. "Heko will wear any resulting scars as badges of honor because she was proud she could represent you in the Games and win the sash for you."

Heko stirred. "Sash . . ."

Taine touched Heko's arm. "I'll take care of it. You rest."

Taine went to the delicate cushioned chair that held Heko's neatly stacked leathers. She pulled the purple-and-black striped sash from the pouch and returned to Heko's bed.

"Heko was going to give this to you tonight," Taine said. "So you'll remember to always fight for what you want in your life." She laid the sash over Zandar's hand.

Zandar stared down at it, stunned. "But . . ."

"She won it for you." Taine knew she straddled a fine line, but it was also the truth. If Zandar knew as much about Emoria as Heko thought she did, she'd know how to take the statement.

Zandar wrapped her fingers around the sash and gazed down at Heko. "It's the most wonderful gift anyone has ever given to me."

TAINE'S ADMIRATION OF Heko's patience grew with each sandmark in the coach to Artocia. She had thought it was good fortune that, after Heko's demonstration of Emoran skills, she was allowed to guard Zandar without joining the Auxies. Now she wasn't sure if she'd be able to survive the trip back all by herself. She should have paid more attention when Heko tried to explain her meditation techniques when they were twelve.

"So you and Nohi are going to be joined?" Zandar asked.

"Yeah," Taine said.

"So, uh, you were the one who, uh . . ."

Taine arched an eyebrow. "Made the first move?"

"Yeah." Zandar straightened but still looked hesitant. "So you just, uh . . ."

"Kissed her?" Taine grinned. "Oh, yeah. Scary but worth it."

"Is it true, if a warrior isn't . . . interested, she'll refuse the kiss?" Zandar focused on her boots.

"Yes," Taine said.

"Then how do you . . . ?"

"Just kiss her."

Zandar lifted her eyes and met Taine's steady gaze. She then seemed to look inward. She nodded and stared out the window.

Taine let out a long breath. Some things were much easier in Emoria.

# Chapter 14

HEKO WISHED SHE hadn't been so groggy and miserable when she gave in to Nara's request to, at least, send word to Hyek and Niko about the incident. She knew her mothers needed to know what had happened to her. Since she was recovering nicely, and the beating looked worse than it actually was, Nara had promised not to go into too much detail.

She should have known her mothers didn't care about how minor the incident, they worried and needed to see the situation for themselves. Fortunately, the healer allowed her to be moved to the safe house. She wasn't ready for the two worlds she found herself in to collide. Not yet.

She adjusted the pillows behind her so she could sit up a little straighter. She frowned at the books piled on the floor, but it was too late for Taine to get them out of sight. Why was she worried about them anyway? She'd been forced to stay in bed for four weeks. She would have gone crazy without them.

The problem was Zandar had lent her the books, and she just wasn't sure if she was able to talk about her, even in a casual way. But she knew she had to talk about her because her mothers were going to want to know why she wanted to stay in Balderon.

She heard several footfalls on the steps and down the corridor. Before she had a chance to brace herself, Hyek and Niko filled the doorway. She frowned at their expressions when they saw her. She didn't look that bad—did she?

Her mothers rushed to her, gave her hugs and kisses on the cheek. Hyek held her face between her hands and studied her eyes for several heartbeats. Then she sat in one of the chairs next to the bed. Niko ran her hand across Heko's cheek and sank into the chair next to Hyek.

Hyek brushed the hair off of Heko's forehead and smiled when it fell back. "How are you?"

"I'm doing fine," Heko said.

"Your lungs—"

"Almost healed." Heko prayed she wouldn't have a coughing fit. They weren't as frequent but they still happened.

"Spells can be tricky," Hyek said.

"Nara brought in the best wizard in Balderon," Heko said. "She found the weave of the spell and agreed with the wizard the doctor had consulted. It'll wear off if I don't aggravate it."

"Looks like you found a way to keep busy while having to stay in bed." Niko picked up a book. "The history of Ynit. Excellent book."

Heko bit down her relief—glad the books not on military history were at the bottom the piles.

Hyek gave her a sidelong look. "When I let you come here, I never suspected you'd get into a position to get beaten up."

"Uh . . ." Heko sighed.

"According to everyone around here," Hyek said with a glint of humor in her eyes, "it's because of a merchant's daughter."

So much for not talking about Zandar. Heko willed her cheeks not to turn pink, but knew they did.

Niko took her hand. "Taine and Nohi like her, and Nara was impressed by her. But the merchant class has their own rules and ways they do things."

"I know." Heko sighed. "I got caught in the middle of it, but I'd do it again."

Hyek and Niki gave her a sympathetic look.

Hyek patted Heko's arm. "According to Taine, that other merchant wants to court . . ."

"Zandar," Heko said. "And Zandar has been saying no to her for two years."

Hyek smiled. "And you think she's interested in you?"

Heko knew her cheeks were red. "She's . . . she asked Taine about, uh, approaching a warrior."

"How does she even know to ask?" Niko asked.

"She's studying to be a scholar of military history, and she's interested in warrior cultures," Heko said. "She's read a lot about Emoria, and has learned a lot more from me and Taine and Nohi . . . She knows about how we do things."

"And she asked Taine about it?" Hyek rubbed her chin. "How do you know it wasn't just curiosity?"

Heko mentally squirmed. "Uh, because . . . ask Taine and Nohi."

Hyek and Niko chuckled. A motherly chuckle Heko was more than familiar with.

Hyek squeezed Heko's hand. "I know this isn't a comfortable

subject for you, but sometimes you have to forget about being a warrior and tell what you know and what's in your heart."

Heko sighed. "She has asked enough questions and knows enough about us to understand how I'm interpreting her actions toward me."

"Actions?" Hyek prompted.

"Teasing and things like that." Heko picked at her blanket. "She even apologizes sometimes because she knows it makes me uncomfortable."

"This still sounds like a Balderon girl just having fun," Hyek said.

Heko took a deep breath and bit her lip. "When she saw Taine and Nohi at the festival she asked if they were going to tease me about being with her. She knows what that means. She could have said they didn't have any reason to tease, but she didn't. When she asked Taine about how to approach a warrior, Taine said she wasn't asking in a curiosity kind of way. She was serious and hesitant and then stared out the window of the coach for a long time afterward. She's never hesitated about asking questions before . . ." Heko realized that she was rattling on.

"But she was on her way back to Artocia when she asked," Niko said.

"She'll only be gone another moon, and then she'll be back for the summer season," Heko said. "She'll be finished with her classes and will only have a research project to do."

"And she doesn't know you're a princess," Niko said.

"She doesn't know."

"And you don't think it'll matter to her when she finds out?" Niko pressed.

Heko shook her head. "I don't think it will."

Hyek smiled. "We aren't going to deny you the opportunity to follow your heart. If she's the one, Laur will find a way for you to be together. We only ask that you be careful. As you've discovered, the ways out here are different from Emoria, and many people don't share our sense of honor."

"Zandar understands our ways, and she has honor," Heko said. "That's all that matters to me. But I'll be careful."

"That's all that we ask for," Niko said.

Heko took each of their hands. "Thank you for understanding."

"I WISH I got the chance to ask Zandar about the Kuntians." Heko pushed the food around on her plate. "I wish I could get back to normal." Three long weeks after Hyek and Niko's visit, and the healer was still worried about her persistent cough.

"Whatever Zandar knows would still be speculation," Taine said. "And the healer knows what she's doing."

Radle set down her tankard. "What's going on anyway? You asked us to let you know if we noticed a drop off in criminal activity, and it drops off. Like you knew it was going to happen. And then you send a couple of scouts on some secret mission . . . You're not planning to have a war and not invite your good friends the Balderon soldiers, are you?"

"If our suspicions are correct, you'll be the ones in the war," Heko said. "Rather quickly without a chance to plan for it."

"So you know this, how?" Sarie asked.

"What do you know about the ruins north of the city?" Heko asked.

"Ruins?" Sarie frowned. "Oh, you mean the city of Kleawe. No one can go near it."

"Why?"

"Because of the way the city was destroyed," Sarie said. "There was a great battle back in the time when armies used wizards. The final spells that destroyed Kleawe set up barriers around it that prevents anyone from getting close enough to even see it."

Taine, Nohi, and Heko exchanged puzzled looks.

"How long ago were these spells cast?" Taine asked.

"The war was six centuries ago," Sarie said.

"And when was the last time someone tried to visit the city?" Heko asked.

Radle and Sarie looked confused.

"No one goes near it," Radle said. "There are stone markers on the spell boundary. Between this boundary and the barrier is an area where stray spells have been known to strike down anyone foolish enough to go near."

Heko frowned. "Exactly where is this boundary?"

"On top of the plateaus that overlook the city and across the passes into the valley," Sarie said.

Taine leaned across the table. "Are you saying those crumbling pillars on top of that plateau mark some kind of spell boundary?"

Radle's eyes widened. "You've been there?"

Taine fell back against the wall and crossed her arms. "You better be glad we've been there."

"Which brings us back to what's going on," Sarie said.

"We'll know when the scouts get back," Heko said.

Sarie sighed and looked around the common room and then cocked her head at Heko. "This is the first time I've had the privilege of spending time in your quaint establishment. Interesting experience. But do you know what I find really interesting?"

"I know you're going to tell us," Heko said.

"I think it's interesting how everyone treats you like you're in charge." Sarie sat back and crossed her arms.

"Heko's a natural leader," Nohi said.

"Natural leader," Sarie said. "You were the natural leader around here, Nohi."

Nohi turned to Heko. "If Ange and Taler find what you think they're going to find, you're going to have to become yourself again."

Taine put her hand on Heko's arm. "The reason for hiding no longer exists anyway."

Heko studied her plate of food. She had succeeded in doing what she wanted to do by keeping her heritage a secret. Perhaps the time had really come for her to slip back into her princess skin. The odd thing was, she didn't feel as suffocated by the idea as she had when she first came to Balderon. If nothing else, meeting Zandar had given her enough confidence in herself as a person to better handle the part that was royal.

She opened her belt pouch, pulled out her princess braid laced with purple threads, and tied it to her belt.

The Emorans rocked the walls with their cheers.

Sarie and Radle exchanged baffled looks.

"What does that braid mean?" Radle asked.

"It means my cousin's the heir to the Emoran throne," Nohi said.

"Really?" Sarie gave a little laugh. "I guess that's a good reason for everyone to think you're in charge."

"So why didn't you want anyone to know you're a princess?" Radle asked.

Heko tried to hide her pink cheeks in her cup of tea.

"She's always been concerned women are only interested in her because of who she is," Taine said.

Sarie laughed. "And not her roguish good looks?"

Taine grinned. "She's never quite understood about her looks. Anyway, she found possibly the only woman in the Southern Territories who never seemed to notice those roguish good looks and thinks Heko's an Auxie who happens to be from Emoria and fell for her anyway."

"You wouldn't happen to be talking about a certain merchant's daughter would you?" Radle asked.

"The very same," Taine said.

"She certainly was concerned when you were beaten up," Sarie said.

Heko looked up. "What do you mean?"

"The next day she came to headquarters looking for Radle and me," Sarie said. "She remembered us from the festival and knew we were friends of yours. She wanted to know if we had heard who was behind your attack."

"She felt guilty because she thinks she got me in the middle of her problems with Brandle," Heko said.

Sarie shook her head. "She was convinced Brandle was behind it and was angry and upset, so she said things she probably wouldn't have if she were calmer. She said Brandle had no right interfering in what she wanted in her life." Sarie gazed at Heko. "It was clear she meant you. We thought nothing of it, because she certainly didn't treat you like a guard at the festival."

Heko sat back stunned.

"In case you had any doubts about that little conversation in the coach," Taine said.

Heko looked down at her hands. "All I had was hope."

Rapid footfalls from the narrow corridor to the front door captured the attention of everyone in the chamber. Ange and Taler rushed in and then walked quickly to Heko's table. They looked like they had seen Bal's Ghost.

"Sit down and tell us," Heko said.

They squeezed onto the bench next to Radle and gratefully accepted tankards of ale from Lise.

"When we got there, three regiments were just starting south, following Feindor Valley," Ange said.

"If you want to get south fast, that's the way to do it," Nohi said.

"Only three?" Heko asked.

Taler shook her head. "That's what took us so long, we got close enough to overhear their commanders, who just happened to be on the plateau watching the troops. They have twelve regiments in all."

Heko sat forward. "Twelve?"

"Right," Taler said. "The first three regiments left three nights ago. To capture the second largest concentration of Territory soldiers."

"In Artocia," Heko said around a sudden lump in her throat.

"Right." Taler gave her a sympathetic look. "The other six regiments left two nights ago. They're skirting the desert, one will go south of Ynit and the other to the east."

"And the one that left tonight will cover the north," Heko said. "A traditional Kuntic tactic is to enter towns disguised as merchants and visitors just passing through and disable the local peacekeeping force as the main regiments move in. Feindor Valley is isolated enough that they only had to deal with tiny villages. And they're moving at night, which means they'll have Ynit surrounded and Artocia taken before the soldiers know they're there."

Sarie rose to her feet, reached across the table, and grabbed Heko's arm. "Kuntics? Regiments? What are you saying?"

The surrounding Emorans tensed and put their hands on their belt knives.

"Uh, Sarie, it's really not a good idea to grab our princess like that," Taine said.

Sarie looked around, released Heko, and sat back down. "Sorry."

"I wanted to find out who was behind all the criminal activity since the last war," Heko said. "While we were out exploring the countryside, we discovered what looked to be a Kuntic settlement in those ruins north of the city."

"Why didn't you report it?" Radle asked.

"Actually I did," Nohi said with a shrug. "To your commander. I was told it wasn't possible for anyone to be in the ruins, and perhaps I had consumed a bit too much of the fabled Emoran ale." She lifted her tankard and took a sip.

Sarie put her head in her hands. "And even if our commander believed you, we wouldn't have been able to do anything about it because of the spells."

"If I had known the reason why no one went near the ruins," Nohi said, "I would have told the commander the spells seem to be gone now."

Sarie looked up. "Gone?"

"Yes," Heko said. "That's how we found the settlement. Because the Kuntics had to be up to something, we decided to keep an eye on them."

"Makes sense," Sarie said.

"We also thought they were behind the criminal activity," Heko said. "It kept the local forces occupied while they were building their army."

"Which leaves us with twelve regiments surrounding Ynit," Taine said.

"And taking over Artocia." Heko stood up.

"I know what you're thinking," Taine said.

Heko looked at Sarie and Radle. "It's your war. Emoria stays neutral until I've had the chance to rescue Zandar from Artocia."

The Emorans, except Taine and Nohi, jumped to their feet and cheered and clapped. Heko held up her hands for silence.

"Once I've accomplished that little mission, I'll petition the queen to allow us to join in the fun."

The cheering echoed off the walls.

"THE HEALER HASN'T released you yet." Nara planted herself in the doorway of Heko and Taine's room.

"I've released myself." Heko turned to Taine. "She's your height, your leathers should fit her."

"We need a scabbard and sword," Taine said.

"Heko." Nara stepped into the chamber and crossed her arms.

Heko and Taine stopped their packing and turned to Nara.

"What would you do if you were in my position?" Heko asked.

"She hasn't even let you know she's interested," Nara said.

"That doesn't change how I feel about her," Heko said. "And even if she isn't interested, I would still go get her."

Nara relaxed her arms. "I know I can't stop you. But remember who you are, and don't take any chances beyond the obvious dangers you'll be putting yourself in."

"I'll be careful," Heko said. "We'll all be careful."

"At least my levelheaded daughter will be going with you," Nara said.

Taine grinned. "She just doesn't want to miss out on the fun."

# Chapter 15

TAINE PULLED THE wagon to a stop just outside the north gate of Artocia a good sandmark after sundown.

A black-uniformed guard stepped in front of the wagon and held up a hand. "Halt."

Another black-uniformed soldier approached the wagon. She looked first at Taine and Nohi on the bench seat, and then Heko on a leather-covered heap in the back.

"Papers." The soldier held out her hand.

Taine, Nohi, and Heko handed over their papers.

The soldier took her time looking at each set of papers. She raised her eyes and studied Taine and Nohi, then glanced at the bundle Heko sat on. "What is your purpose here?"

"We're delivering an order of swords and daggers," Nohi said.

"Swords." The soldiers exchanged glances. "Who made this order?"

Taine pulled a scroll from her belt pouch and handed it to the soldier.

The soldier read it and passed it to her companion. "Fortunately for you, our commander's name's on that order."

"Emorans are neutral," Nohi said.

"Only until you decide not to be." The soldier handed back their papers and the blades order.

"At the moment we're neutral," Nohi said, "and it seems to be to your advantage."

Taine shook the reins, and the wagon lumbered through the gate.

The city was eerily quiet, except for soldiers stationed on corners and patrolling the streets. Most every window was filled with light—the citizens were probably too afraid to darken their homes.

"I wonder what happened to the Territory soldiers," Heko said in a low voice.

Taine and Nohi looked back at her.

"Don't get any more ideas," Taine said. "We're going to be lucky to get Zandar out of here. Anyway, we can't interfere until we declare which side we're on."

"I know." Heko shrugged. "I hope the soldiers in Ynit have mobilized."

"We can worry about that when we get back to Balderon." Nohi pointed down a narrow road, and Taine guided the wagon around the corner.

Heko sighed and put her elbows on her knees. "Living around you is like having an older sister."

Nohi flashed Heko a grin. "I'll take that as a compliment. Down the next alley."

Taine turned the corner into a narrow alley and stopped next to a covered forge.

Heko jumped out of the wagon and slung a small pack over her shoulder. "I'll be back as quickly as possible."

Taine and Nohi climbed off the wagon.

Nohi grasped Heko's shoulder. "Good luck, and don't take any chances."

"Don't leave us with the task of having to tell Hyek bad news," Taine said.

"Don't worry," Heko said. "Just do what you need to do here."

"No problem—as long as we use your name." Nohi grinned at Heko's look of resignation. "Remember, you have to tell her who you are before you get to the safe house."

Heko nodded. "I will. See you later."

She ghosted down the alley and waited for a pair of soldiers to cross the street and walk in the direction away from the university.

She kept to the shadows and trotted down the road, thanking Laur the safe house was only a few blocks from the university. She wasn't surprised to see soldiers guarding the main gate to the grounds and didn't doubt the patrols were heavy along the surrounding wall. She grinned as she followed the shadows to the wall and waited a few heartbeats while she opened her senses for anyone nearby. She then climbed up and dropped to the other side.

The grounds of the university were anything but quiet, and the buildings were ablaze with light both outside and inside. Heko quickly strolled past the buildings where students and scholars were gathered on steps and in courtyards engaged in spirited discussions. They were obviously not allowed to leave the grounds.

She scanned the students as she passed by, but knew, as much as she would like it to be, Zandar wasn't among them. The university administrators would have made sure the offspring of merchants remained safely inside.

With some relief, She finally saw Zandar's building. As she trotted up the steps, she realized she didn't even know how to find Zandar's room.

"Whoa. That's what I call a warrior," a woman said.

Heko stopped and turned to a group of students gathered on the main staircase.

"You can take me hostage any time," a young woman said.

"I'm looking for Zandar," Heko said.

"I'd make a much better hostage." The young woman waggled her eyebrows.

"Zandar's a friend," Heko said.

"I'll have to compliment Zandar on her taste in friends then," the young woman said.

"Please, where's her room?" Heko asked.

"Second floor. Turn left. It's the last one on the right." The student gave Heko a sly grin as she pushed past the group. "Nice muscles."

Heko rolled her eyes as she hurried up the steps and down the corridor. The door was open, and she paused on the threshold. Zandar was curled up on a chair in front of the fire, reading a book. The whole world had been turned upside down around her, and she was calmly reading.

Heko gently rapped on the door. Zandar blinked up and then stumbled to her feet.

"Heko." Zandar rushed across the room and threw herself into a startled Heko's arms.

Zandar's sudden warmth left Heko lightheaded and without thinking, she wrapped her arms around her.

After several heartbeats, Zandar pulled away just enough to look up into Heko's eyes. "I'm so happy to see you."

Heko stared into Zandar's eyes and felt as if she was drowning in an ocean of glistening blue. Mesmerized, she forgot to be nervous, forgot to be frightened, and would have been dumbfounded if someone told her she actually met Zandar halfway. The only thing she knew was if she survived all the sweet sensations from Zandar's lips pressed against hers she would never be able to live without those lips on hers again.

"You didn't reject me," Zandar said in a voice thick with emotion.

Heko, dazed and trying to steady her breathing, shook her head. "Never." Her heart almost stopped at Zandar's radiant smile.

"Why are you here?" Zandar asked. "Come sit down. You look like you're about to keel over." She grabbed Heko's arm, pulled her to the chair in front of the fire, and knelt in front of her.

"We're here to rescue you," Heko said.

Zandar grasped Heko's hands. "You came all the way here just for me?"

Heko blinked at her. "Of course. I couldn't leave you in any kind of danger."

Zandar gazed into Heko eyes. "Lucky for me, Emorans still possess the souls of heroes."

Heko frowned. "This has nothing to do with heroics."

Zandar kissed Heko's cheek. "I know. But even love in our society no longer brings out such self-sacrifice." She smiled at Heko's confused look. "Brandle claims to love me, but I don't see her here. Many of the students here have lovers, but no one expects them to come and rescue them and I don't think they'd even think of it. That's the job of the local guards and the Territory soldiers."

"You don't deserve to live in such a society then." Heko surprised herself with her bold words, but she owed Zandar nothing less than her true feelings.

Zandar cocked her head. "Is that the way an Emoran warrior asks an outsider to join with her?"

Heko gazed down at their clasped hands. "I don't know. That's a private matter not talked about. But in Emoria, the warrior and the woman she's interested in would have spent enough time with each other and would have sent enough signals to each other so when the woman shows interest, she's letting the warrior know she wants to be joined with her." She swallowed and looked up at Zandar. "But I know that things work differently out here—"

Zandar stopped Heko's words with a heartfelt kiss. "I understood completely what I was doing when I kissed you. You're all that I've thought about for moons now, and I know I want to spend my life with you." She laughed at Heko's stunned and delighted expression and wrapped her arms around her. "Will your mother have a problem with this?"

"My mother?" Heko frowned in confusion.

Zandar pulled back and lifted the purple threaded braid on Heko's belt. "I noticed the new addition to your belt. I did a lot of research on Emoran culture. This braid represents royal blood." She gave Heko a sympathetic look. "It must be a difficult burden to carry."

"I came to Balderon so I could be an ordinary person, doing ordinary things," Heko said.

"You're too good of a warrior and too noble a soul to be ordinary," Zandar said. "Will your mother have a problem with your being joined to an outsider?"

"She'll love you," Heko whispered.

"I look forward to meeting both your mothers." Zandar squeezed Heko's hands. "Now I'm bursting with curiosity. How did you get through that army?"

Heko chuckled. "Taine, Nohi, and I put together a wagonload of junk swords and daggers and a fake weapons order from the Kuntic commander here and simply rode into town. Emoria is neutral until we take sides."

"How'd you find out the name of the commander?" Zandar asked.

Heko grinned. "We asked when we past the main army north of Ynit."

Zandar burst out laughing. "Clever. And when do you plan to take sides?"

"As soon as we get you back to Balderon," Heko said.

"One more question." Zandar gave Heko an impish grin. "How do you plan to get me back to Balderon?"

Heko picked her pack up off the floor and pulled out a set of Emoran leathers. "You're going to find out what it's like to be an Emoran."

Zandar's eyes widened. "I don't think putting those on will convince anyone I'm Emoran."

"You'll look fine," Heko said. "These are Taine's leathers. They should fit you well enough."

"Except she has muscles—everywhere."

Heko smiled and put the leathers into Zandar's arms. "I'll step outside while you change." She stood and pulled Zandar up with her.

"You'll have to explain to me sometime how a country full of women can go through life without ever seeing each other naked, except when they're joined," Zandar said.

"Uh." Heko looked at her feet. "I'll be in the corridor." She trotted to the door as Zandar's affectionate laugh followed her.

"NOHI?" A SMALL, muscular woman stepped out of the door inside the forge. "What in Laur's name is going on?"

"Hey, Aunt Neri," Nohi said. "We'll explain. Inside."

"Does your mother know you're here?" Neri asked over her shoulder as she walked back into the shop.

Taine and Nohi rolled their eyes at each other and followed her.

"Yes, she knows," Nohi said. "We're on a mission."

"Mission?" Neri's voice was laced with skepticism. "More like young warriors wanting to play war."

"Really. We're here to help my cousin."

Neri stopped at the entrance to the narrow corridor and faced Nohi. "Cousin? Since I know Nena isn't in need of help, you must be referring to your other cousin." She crossed her arms.

"Heko," Nohi said. "We're here to rescue her future life companion. A student at the university."

Neri looked surprised then she shook her head and walked down the corridor. "Come. You must be hungry and tired. You can tell me about it while you eat."

The brightness of the common room was blinding after the darkened city. The room was filled with Emorans who looked at them with curiosity. They certainly didn't look like they were in the middle of an occupied city.

"An odd time to pick for a visit." A young woman stood up from a table and put her hands on her hips.

Taine did a double take. The tall Emoran had more than a passing resemblance to Heko.

Nohi grinned. "I just wanted to show off my future life companion to the rest of my family."

"Then all your good sense has leaked out of your ears." The young woman strolled around the tables and pulled Nohi into a hug.

"This is Taine," Nohi said. "Taine, meet my other cousin, Nena."

"Well met, Nena," Taine said.

"Well met, Taine," Nena said. "You're actually from Emoria."

"The accent gives me away every time," Taine said.

"Now sit down and tell us why you're really here." Nena led the way around the tables of gawking Emorans to a table where a couple of young women cleared a place for them.

Taine and Nohi gratefully accepted plates of stew and bread and spiced tea.

"We're here to rescue Heko's future life companion," Nohi said. "She's a student at the university."

Nena frowned. "An Emoran?"

"A citizen of Balderon," Nohi said.

"And how do you plan to rescue her?" Neri asked. "The university is surrounded by soldiers."

Nohi grinned. "The best tracker in Emoria is getting her as we speak."

Neri raised surprised eyebrows. "The best tracker."

"Heko." Nohi scooped a forkful of food into her mouth.

"Are you saying our princess is out there sneaking around all those soldiers?" Neri asked, flabbergasted. "Have you all lost your senses?"

Taine shrugged. "Maybe. But nothing would keep Heko from getting Zandar safely back to Balderon."

"How are you planning to leave the city?" Neri asked.

"How'd you get into the city?" Nena asked. "They're not letting anyone in."

Nohi shrugged as she took a sip of tea. "We got in with a wagonload of junk swords and a fake order for weapons from the Kuntian commander."

The surrounding, shamelessly eavesdropping Emorans laughed.

"That sounds like something The Trickster would come up with," Neri said.

"She can be very creative when she's focused," Taine said.

Neri sighed. "No doubt she'll make a good queen—if she lives that long."

"She will," Nohi said. "Zandar will see to it."

"An outsider?" Nena took a long sip of ale. "How can an outsider understand anything about Emorans or Emoria?"

Taine and Nohi looked at each other and laughed.

"She's a military historian with an interest in Emoria," Nohi said. "She's probably the only woman on earth who truly understands Heko."

"Is it true that our princess is . . . uh . . . very striking looking?" Nena asked.

They all turned at voices and shuffling from the narrow corridor leading to the front door.

"I think you're about to find out for yourself," Nohi said.

The older Emoran who was on door watch emerged from the corridor and looked back with a kind of awestruck expression.

Heko slipped past the woman, and the room stilled as every pair of eyes gazed at her in stunned admiration.

Taine leaned close to Nohi. "Emoran leathers really do bring out the best in our princess."

Heko looked back and gently pulled Zandar into the room.

Zandar fussed with a sleeve of her leathers, then she gazed around the room and frowned.

"Everyone's staring at you," she said in a low voice.

Heko sighed. "Welcome to my world."

She led the way around the tables to Taine and Nohi. Several Emorans got up to allow them to pass.

Neri and Nena rose to their feet as Heko approached.

Nohi sat back and grinned. "Heko, meet your other aunt and cousin. Neri, Nena, meet the black sheep of the family."

The surrounding Emorans laughed and relaxed.

"Well met, Neri. Well met, Nena," Heko said.

"Well met, my princess," Neri said.

Nena grinned. "Well met, cousin."

Heko returned the grin. "This is Zandar. She thinks she looks ridiculous in our leathers."

"You do my leathers proud, Zandar," Taine said.

Neri bowed her head with respect. "Well met, Zandar."

Zandar looked surprised. "Well met, Neri."

"Well met, Zandar." Nena also bowed her head.

"Well met, Nena." A confused Zandar turned to Heko who gazed down at her boots.

Nohi stood and put a friendly arm around Zandar's shoulders. "I think you'd better get used to being treated with awe and respect for a while."

Zandar looked even more confused.

Nohi chuckled. "Sit. Have you eaten?" Zandar shook her head. She gently pushed Zandar down onto the bench and sat Heko next to her.

"Nohi acts like a big sister," Heko said.

Everyone else took their seats at the table, and servers put steaming plates of stew and bread in front of Heko and Zandar.

"So did you have any problems with your valiant rescue?" Taine asked.

Zandar swallowed a mouthful of stew. "Heko had the worst time fighting off several of my classmates."

After a heartbeat of stunned silence the room erupted in laughter. Taine and Nohi were laughing so hard at Heko's expression they couldn't catch their breaths.

Neri reached over the table and patted Zandar's hand. "You're going to fit in just fine."

Taine wiped her eyes. "You mean you didn't jump in to protect her?"

"Actually, I told them to get their own and leave mine alone," Zandar said.

Heko put her face in her hands and shook her head.

"You know, Heko," Taine said. "The more I'm around Zandar, the more I'm liking her."

Heko uncovered her face and looked at Zandar. "Can I unrescue you?"

Zandar gave her a dazzling grin.

"You're opening yourself up to a lifetime of teasing," Taine said.

Heko blinked away from gazing at Zandar and returned her attention to her plate.

Zandar playfully bumped Heko with her shoulder, and they both smiled as they ate.

"So you're just going to ride out of town tomorrow?" Neri asked.

"Yep," Nohi said. "We'll leave the junk swords and daggers with you and take the empty wagon back."

"What about the extra Emoran with you?" Neri asked.

"She was visiting family here, and we're taking her back to Balderon," Nohi said.

Zandar dug into her belt pouch and pulled out a document. "I have the papers to prove it."

"Forged," Neri said.

"Real." Heko pulled a chain out from under her leathers. The royal seal of Emoria dangled from it. "I took the liberty of making Zandar a citizen of Emoria, since it's going to happen soon enough anyway."

"You didn't know that when you put the seal to those papers," Zandar said.

"I was hopeful."

"Heko was so desperate she was ready to forget Emoran tradition, forget her stoic warrior upbringing, and beg Zandar to be joined with her." Taine somehow managed to stand and back away as Heko jumped to her feet and unsheathed her sword.

Heko pointed the sword at Taine's heart. "I'm only going to spare your life because I don't want to dry Nohi's mournful tears."

Nohi stumbled to her feet. "Hey. We made a pact we wouldn't tease each other."

Neri put her hands on her hips. "What kind of nonsense is that?"

Heko shrugged and sheathed her sword. "The rules of teasing changed to allow for an outsider."

Taine grinned and crossed her arms. "Welcome to the family, Zandar."

# Chapter 16

TAINE OPENED THE door and almost laughed at Nohi's expression. "Are you still angry with Neri?"

"She didn't have to treat us like children," Nohi said.

Zandar stepped up behind Taine and muffled a laugh. "Even after, let's see, Taine levels the ultimate insult at Heko, Heko pulls a sword on Taine, and then you spend the next half sandmark explaining your revision of the time-honored rules of teasing between warriors to Neri? I'm surprised she didn't make us sleep with the horses."

Heko stepped into the corridor from the room opposite Taine and Zandar's.

"She didn't have to keep checking to make sure we were in the right rooms," Nohi said with a scowl.

"You know the traditions are tighter for royals," Taine said. "And with Zandar being an outsider, raised with more lenient attitudes . . ."

Zandar slipped past Taine and went to Heko. They grinned at each other.

Nohi rolled her eyes. "It doesn't help they're making the trees jealous with their sappy looks."

Taine shook her head and grabbed Nohi's arm. "Come in here." She pulled Nohi into the room and out of sight.

Zandar wrapped her arms around Heko's neck. "Shall we indulge in some of that lenient attitude?"

Heko surrendered to Zandar's soft lips.

"You never told me Heko snores," Nohi said from within the room.

Heko and Zandar put their foreheads together and could only laugh.

"Heko does not snore," Taine said.

"Nohi's a little nervous about this mission," Heko whispered in Zandar's ear. "She's feeling the pressure of being the eldest and being unbraided as a warrior. Her skills haven't been tested yet."

"But aren't you her leader?" Zandar asked.

"If I forced it, she'd have to follow my orders," Heko said. "But she's the one who would be responsible if something happened to me—at least for another week until I turn eighteen."

Zandar brightened. "Your birthday is next week?"

"Yes."

"I heard snoring." Nohi walked to the door. Heko stepped away from Zandar, and they tried to look innocent.

"You heard wheezing," Taine said.

Zandar gazed at Heko. "You're not completely healed?"

Heko sighed. "I'm fine. Just a bit of a cough and some congestion."

Zandar threw her hands up in frustration. "Congestion? You risked aggravating a spell you don't know anything about . . ."

Heko grabbed Zandar's hands and pulled them to her heart. Zandar blinked up at her. "You know nothing would have kept me from coming here to get you. Taine and Nohi know that. They would do the same for each other. You're not allowed to feel any guilt about this."

Zandar glared at her, outraged. "I'll feel what I want to feel, Heko Ketlas, heir to the Emoran throne."

Heko stared wide-eyed at her, then glanced at Taine and Nohi, who looked both stunned and amused.

"Excuse us," she mumbled as she dragged a confused Zandar into the other room. She closed the door with her shoulder, wrapped her arms around Zandar, and pulled her into a heartfelt kiss. "Thank you. And don't ever change."

Breathless from the kiss, Zandar gazed at Heko, taking in the gentle blue eyes and rakish tousled hair. "You don't like being a princess do you?"

"Don't ever tell anyone," Heko said. "Until I met you, all I wanted to be was a warrior. Now all I want to be is with you. I'd be content to stand beside you while you pursue being a scholar, a teacher, a merchant . . . whatever you want to be."

Zandar gathered Heko's hands into hers and pulled them to her heart. "Until I met you, all I wanted to be was a scholar of military history and teacher at a university. Now all I want is to be with you. Before we go back out there and before you have to play stoic Emoran warrior who doesn't show affection in public, I just want to say I love you so much that I'm about to burst from it."

Zandar's breath caught as Heko's eyes glistened, and a tear rolled down her cheek.

She gently brushed the tear away. "I've read Emoran warriors don't cry."

"They don't," Heko said. "Not in public. What warriors do in private is never spoken of." She took Zandar's hand and pressed it to her lips. "But as far as I know, warriors can just be themselves in private with their life companion. With the person they love."

They jumped from a knock on the door.

"I can hear Neri coming this way," Nohi said through the door.

Heko sighed, stepped away from Zandar, and opened the door.

"It's going to be fun around you two," Taine said.

Heko frowned as she and Zandar walked into the corridor. "What does that mean?"

Taine only grinned.

Neri topped the steps and crossed her arms, but smiled at them. "I hope you plan to have a good meal before you bluff your way past that army all the way back to Balderon."

"Of course," Nohi said. "Uh, we were kind of hoping you'd let us raid the larder for some cheese and bread to take along."

"As if I'd say no to my own nieces," Neri said. "And one of them my princess."

"She doesn't like to be treated like a princess," Nohi said.

Neri walked up to Heko and Nohi. "You both make me proud to be blood-related to you. Promise you'll come back to visit when this little problem of an invading army is taken care of."

Heko looked at Zandar. "I'll be here while Zandar finishes her studies."

After the words they had just exchanged, Zandar shouldn't have been surprised but she was. A part of her still thought Heko's independence would be reined in by her station in life. She knew she wasn't supposed to embarrass Heko in public with something as innocent as a hug, so she returned Heko's smile.

"Hyek isn't going to know what to make of that," Neri said, "but I'm sure she'll accept any decision you make."

Heko shrugged. "Who knows. Maybe all this learning around here will rub off."

"YOU'RE THE QUEEN'S only daughter?" Zandar pulled her knees to her chin as she tried to get a bit more comfortable in the back of the wagon. Heko sat cross-legged against the side panel opposite her.

Taine and Nohi sat on the bench seat in front as they rolled on a rutted dirt road just north of the desert.

"Yep." Heko was just happy she could openly watch Zandar on this trip back from Artocia.

"And Nohi is your cousin—"

"My birth mother, Niko, is Nohi's mother's sister," Heko said.

Zandar frowned. "So, you're not actually related to the queen by blood?"

Heko's confusion mirrored Zandar's until she remembered Zandar couldn't possibly know how Emorans conceived. "There are some things outsiders don't know about Emorans. We, uh, don't conceive in the same way."

Zandar's eyebrows shot up. "I don't understand."

"Uh. All right. Let's take your mother." Heko had promised herself that she wouldn't keep anything from Zandar, no matter how hard it was to explain. She took a deep breath. "Was she ever joined to a man?"

"No," Zandar said. "She's always been attracted to women. She's actually joined to Arbiter Ginle, but they separated last year, and will probably have their joining annulled."

Heko stared wide-eyed at her. "Annulled?"

Zandar gave her a curious look. "Don't you have annulments in Emoria?"

"Annulments?"

"If two people decide they no longer want to be joined they can have their joining annulled," Zandar said. "It doesn't happen a lot, but it happens often enough that it's not considered uncommon."

Heko's mouth fell open as she tried to process the foreignness of the idea. "Why . . . why would they no longer want to be joined?"

"Many reasons. Some just fall out of love or never really loved each other in the first place. Sometimes it's infidelity—"

"Infidelity?" Heko was beyond shocked. "You mean they actually become . . . intimate with someone other than their life companion?"

Zandar took Heko's hand. "I'm glad the ideas of annulment and infidelity are unheard of in Emoria." She released Heko's hand and sat back. "Now you were trying to explain how Emorans have children."

Heko nodded, happy to not think about the disquieting practices in the outside world. "When your mother and her partner wanted to have children, they had to, uh, enlist the help of a male."

"Right." Zandar drew out the word.

"We don't."

"Don't what?"

"Use males," Heko said.

"She's not going to believe you," Nohi said over her shoulder.

Heko gazed at Zandar. "I know it doesn't sound possible but Laur blesses a couple with a child."

"Blesses," Zandar said.

Heko bit her lip as she searched for the words. "We don't have annulments because Laur doesn't allow a false joining. She can read our hearts, and knows when a love is true and forever. When she feels a couple is ready, one is chosen to be the birth mother and is prepared to receive the seed of a child into her body. When her body is prepared, she and her partner, uh, perform a ceremony that allows both of them to contribute to the seed."

Zandar blinked at her then looked at the backs of Taine and Nohi, who seemed to be focused on the road ahead. She looked back at Heko and then crawled across the wagon bed to sit cross-legged in front of her—touching knee-to-knee. "I'm sorting through the hundreds of questions I have." She kept her voice low.

Heko let out her breath in relief.

"First, I'm a little concerned about how Laur feels about outsiders."

Heko chuckled and glanced at Taine and Nohi to make sure they couldn't hear them over the rumble of the wheels on the rough road. "She's already accepted you."

"How do you know?" Zandar asked.

Heko leaned forward. "Because she wouldn't let just anyone kiss the heir to the throne," she whispered in Zandar's ear.

Zandar pulled back. "Really?"

Heko smiled, letting her affection show through. "Really."

"I know in my heart I want to spend my life with you," Zandar said. "But I've seen friends who thought they were madly in love, and they are now just as madly out of love."

"We have crushes growing up, even get romantically involved rather young sometimes," Heko said. "Taine's had some experience with that. But we don't get serious until we feel we're old enough for a lifelong commitment."

Zandar's expression turned playful. "So was one of Taine's crushes on you?"

Heko glanced at Taine's back and lowered her voice. "Once—but only in passing. We've been close friends since we were six. We figured out early that we weren't meant to be life companions. We're what we call blood sisters—as close as real sisters."

"She doesn't have a real sister either?" Zandar asked.

"No. And yes, we do tend to adopt sisters if we're an only child," Heko said. "Laur is rather stingy with the blessing of children. Most couples have only one daughter, some have two. A few with three daughters."

Zandar nodded. "So there's a lot of sisterly bonding between girls who don't become life companions."

"Yeah." Heko was distracted by the way the sun played with Zandar's sparkling blue eyes.

Zandar grinned. "You'd better be careful. You don't want to be teased."

"I'll take the risk," Heko whispered, mesmerized by having Zandar so close and filled with wonder that she felt so comfortable with her.

"I'm not seeing this," Taine said.

Heko and Zandar looked at the front of the wagon. Taine put her hand over her eyes.

"We're just talking," Heko said.

"Talking, huh?" Taine said. "Just let me know when your discussion is over so I don't have to lie to our friends back in Emoria when they fill me full of ale in hopes of stories about you two."

Heko grinned. "They know better than to get you to tell stories about me."

Taine turned around and met Heko's amused look. "I hate it when you're right." She threw up her hands in mock defeat. "Now just pretend we're not here and stare into each other's eyes and murmur endearments and kiss and hold hands. Laur knows you deserve the time together in the middle of all this craziness. Who knows when you'll have it again."

Zandar cocked her head at Heko. "You know, the more I see of Taine the more I like her."

Nohi snorted, and Taine looked as if she wasn't quite sure if she liked her words turned around on her.

"Better be careful, she's smarter than all of us," Heko said.

"Yeah, yeah." Taine grinned and faced the road.

Heko leaned forward and kissed Zandar. "My respect for my fellow warriors has soared. All I want to do is hold and kiss you and stare into your beautiful eyes and thank Laur she allowed me to find you."

"It's just enough to know that you feel that way when you have to act like a tough stoic warrior," Zandar said.

Heko didn't think she could ever be any happier than she was at that moment.


TAINE SUCKED IN her breath, pulled out her courage, and walked into the open from behind a large boulder.

Three soldiers in the uniforms of the Southern Territories appeared on the lip of rocks that hid the end of a hollow in the hills north of Ynit on the edge of the desert.

"Identify yourself," one of the soldiers said.

"Taine, Emoran scout." She held out her papers.

The soldier approached and took them at arm's length. She held them close to her eyes in the dying light of the day. "What is your business here?"

"There are four of us with a wagon," Taine said. "All we ask is to spend the night in the safe protection of your camp."

The soldier turned and nodded to her companion who turned and executed a series of arm signals. Within heartbeats, a soldier with the sash of commander on her sleeve emerged from behind the rocks and strode to Taine.

She stopped a pace away and studied Taine. The soldier handed her the papers, which she read. "Not that I know much about the activities of Emorans, but it seems odd for you to be out here, surrounded by an invading army."

"Our princess's future life companion is a student at Artocia," Taine said. "She wanted to rescue her in the short window of time Emoria remains neutral in this conflict."

"Emoria is going to take sides?" the commander asked.

"Yes," Taine said. "Our princess has been living in Balderon, and her future life companion is from Balderon. She wants to help defend the Southern Territories from these invaders."

"This wouldn't happen to be the same Emoran who beat Kiki at Balderon's festival?"

"Yes." Taine sent a quick prayer to Laur that Kiki wasn't a favorite in Ynit and hid her relief when the commander's eyes sparkled in amusement.

"She's with you now?" the commander asked.

"Yes," Taine said.

"Then it'll be a pleasure to salute the person who wiped that boastful smirk from Kiki's face," the commander said.

Taine grinned, turned to the field of boulders behind her, and waved. Heko and Zandar stepped out from behind a boulder followed by Nohi on the wagon.

The commander and the soldiers stared at Heko as if mesmerized as she walked to them. Taine had to admit she cut a striking figure in the waning light.

Zandar turned to Heko. "They're staring at you."

Taine laughed. "You'd better get used to that."

The commander gave her head a shake. "I'm commander Melie. Welcome to our camp. I have the feeling you have some knowledge of this army that can be of use to us."

"We'll tell you everything we know," Heko said.

# Chapter 17

ZANDAR COULDN'T KEEP from staring wide-eyed as they walked through the camp in the surprisingly long and wide hollow. All her reading about field military camps couldn't prepare her for the smells and sounds and tents and soldiers—everywhere.

Heko took Zandar's arm. "You're staring."

Zandar blinked at her and then playfully punched her arm. "Not the same as all these soldiers stopping everything to stare as you walk by."

Heko quickly looked around and turned her attention to the ground. "Why do they do that?" she muttered.

Zandar laughed. "But seriously, this is a major camp."

"It seems the soldiers of the Southern Territories got the Council to give them this camp and a regiment as a hidden reserve," Heko said. "We discovered it when we cut across country to get to Artocia."

Zandar gave her a knowing look. "Without them discovering you?"

Heko shrugged. "We are the best scouts and trackers."

"We rarely get guests but we keep a tent just in case," Melie said as she led them to a tent nestled against one of the towering bluff walls.

Taine looked up at the surrounding stone. "Reminds me a bit of home."

They followed Melie into the tent where she lit a lamp on a table. Several bed rolls were lined up against the back. Melie turned to Heko. "We usually don't get royalty. We can have pallets brought in . . ."

Heko chuckled. "I spent my life training to be a warrior. I've spent many a night sleeping on the plain ground. A bed roll will be a luxury."

Melie nodded. "The mess is along the other bluff. We start serving the evening meal at seven sandmarks. We'll have a chance to talk about that army then."

"Thank you for everything," Heko said.

"Always a pleasure to help a powerful ally. I'll see all of you later." Melie stepped out of the tent.

Nohi looked around. "Beats sleeping in the wagon." She picked up a pair of bed rolls and piled them into Heko's arms. "And Neri isn't here. We'll take that corner. You two can curl up wherever you want."

"Are you sure Nohi's not the princess?" Zandar asked.

Heko shook her head and went to the opposite corner and dropped the bed rolls. "Nohi and Taine are waiting too long to get joined."

Taine put her hands on her hips. "What's that supposed to mean?"

"It means, if you were in Emoria you'd be joined by now," Heko said. "You chose to wait because you wanted to spend the fall and winter in Emoria."

'We didn't want to travel back and forth all the time," Nohi said.

Zandar frowned and turned to Heko. "What about us?"

"Uh . . ." Heko looked at her boots.

Taine laughed. "I suggest you get joined as quickly as possible."

Heko blinked up at her. "What's that supposed to mean?"

"It means any wait is going to be too long for you two." Taine rushed outside the tent before Heko got her hand on the hilt of her sword.

Nohi laughed and turned to Zandar. "Because Heko's a princess, your joining will involve a bit more ceremony."

Heko sighed. "Maybe I can petition for a simple ceremony in the Temple."

"And deny Hyek the honor of overseeing your joining in front of everyone in Emoria?" Nohi said. "No chance."

Zandar's eyes widened. "What?"

Heko turned to her and took her hands. "It's not as bad as it sounds."

Taine stuck her head through the doorway. "The mess is open."

The others grinned and stepped out into the dark, cool air. They followed the soldiers headed toward a long tent.

"That smells great," Nohi said.

"I've never known anyone who likes food as much as you do," Heko said.

"Just an appreciation for the simple pleasures in life," Nohi said.

"Simple . . ." Heko stopped walking and fell to her knees.

"Heko." Zandar dropped to her knees in front of Heko, put her hands on her cheeks, and raised her head.

Heko looked dazed. "I'm all right." She doubled over with a deep, hacking cough.

Taine slid to her knees next to Heko. "Laur's waterfalls, Heko. You're not all right. You said you were all right to take this trip."

"I'm fine," Heko forced out in a hoarse voice. "It's just the cool air."

"Cool air?" Taine worked to keep her anger down. "You grew up in the mountains. This air is as warm as it gets up there."

Heko gazed at her. "This will go away. This spell will wear off."

Taine swallowed as she read the mixture of seriousness and sadness in Heko's eyes. "You're not getting out of standing up for me at my joining."

Heko shook her head without breaking eye contact with Taine. "Not a chance. And you're standing up for me, too."

Taine sucked in a breath. "You're the strongest person I know. It hasn't been easy seeing this kind of weakness."

"I'm only human," Heko said. "Considering what could have happened that night, weak lungs aren't such a bad thing. At least I can work to make them better."

Taine nodded. "Let Zandar take you back to the tent. We'll come back with food and the commander so we can talk to her. If you're going to admit to being human, you'll have to accept that you have to take care of yourself."

Heko nodded and looked at the ground.

Taine and Nohi exchanged alarmed looks.

"What?" Zandar asked.

Taine and Nohi helped Heko to her feet.

Zandar stood. "She's as weak as a kitten."

"She seems to have had a rather major relapse," Nohi said as they turned and walked back to the tent.

"I'll be fine," Heko mumbled. "I just need a good night's rest. Didn't get one last night."

"I hope you're right," Taine said.

They walked into the tent and lowered Heko onto a chair at the table. Melie rushed in after them.

"What happened?" she asked.

"Heko's still recovering from injuries from an accident," Nohi said. "This is the first time she's been out and about in two moons. She doesn't know her limits yet. We were going to bring the food back here and invite you to join us."

"I'll take care of the food." Melie stepped outside the tent.

Zandar sat next to Heko. "Am I allowed to feel some guilt for you being in this condition?"

Heko put her elbows on the table and sighed. "I did a lot of thinking while in that bed . . . and a lot of reading, thanks to the books you lent me." She smiled at Zandar. "When I first came to Artocia, I realized there was so much in the world I didn't know anything about, and I wondered how I could possibly be a good queen."

Taine and Nohi sank onto the other chairs around the table.

"But I also knew Emoria's queens have ruled for as long as we've recorded our history with only what I learned in my warrior training and in my royal tutoring." Heko gave them a sheepish look. "This bothered me until you started asking me about Emoria." She took Zandar's hand. "I discovered even the scholars in Artocia didn't know everything. When I was recuperating I realized I wanted to come to my birthright with as much knowledge as possible. I enjoyed reading the books and learning new things."

"But you're a warrior," Taine said. "The best warrior in Emoria."

"I love being a warrior," Heko said. "But I can live with this," she tapped her chest, "if I have to."

"Really?" Taine asked.

"Yeah." Heko chuckled. "I used to tease you about all those acolytes and scholars who would try to catch your eye. I guess Laur was just waiting to get back at me for that." She squeezed Zandar's hand. "So instead of being guilty, you should feel good that you've given me a chance to expand my world and show me I can be more than a warrior. Meeting you has changed my life in so many wonderful ways, and I'll be forever grateful to you."

Zandar squeezed Heko's hand. "I think I'm at a loss for words."

"When did you grow up?" Taine scratched her head.

"I *am* going to be of legal age in a week," Heko said.

"I know one thing," Taine said. "I don't want to be around when you explain your sudden interest in scholarship to the queen."


HEKO BLINKED AWAKE. She was wrapped in several wool blankets. Another body was close . . . very close. She let her eyes get used to the gray of dawn and gazed in wonder at the beautiful sleeping face surrounded by a tangle of black hair just a couple of hand spans from her own face.

The idea that she would spend the rest of her life waking up and seeing that face next to her stole her breath away. She realized she had a clear breath to be stolen. Her lungs felt fine, and she felt strong and refreshed. Despite her brave words the night before, she prayed to Laur she had all her warrior skills back when she started sparring again.

She widened her eyes when Zandar moved and stretched herself awake. They lay there and just gazed at each other for several heartbeats.

Zandar finally touched Heko's cheek. "How are you feeling?"

"I'm fine." Heko took a deep breath. "No problem."

"Good."

"Did you, uh, sleep well?" Heko asked. "On the ground that is."

"I slept fine. I enjoyed the company." She grinned as Heko felt her cheeks redden.

"You do that on purpose." Heko covered her face with a blanket.

Zandar laughed, pulled the blanket away from Heko's face, and then propped herself up on an elbow. Heko leaned forward and gave Zandar a good morning kiss.

"I look forward to that every morning," Zandar said.

"Every morning forever," Heko whispered.

"For a tough warrior you know how to melt my heart and soul." Zandar leaned in for another kiss.

A crash that sounded like the swords leaning against a tent post clattering to the ground tore their attention from each other.

"Daughter of a shaggy goat," said a frustrated-sounding Taine.

"I don't think Neri would approve of whatever is going on over there," Heko said loud enough for Taine and Nohi to hear her.

Zandar snorted her laughter.

"That's it." A shadow struggled to its feet and bent over to scoop up a sword.

Heko rolled to her feet, grabbed her sword on the way up, and got it in front of her in time to stop Nohi's swing. They slid all the way up to the hilt and stared at each other in the dim light.

"Glad to see you feeling better," Nohi said as she backed away.

"I feel fine," Heko said.

Taine got up and walked to the tent opening. "Nice morning."

Zandar stood up and ran her hand through her hair. "This whole idea of not being afraid of swords is going to take getting used to."

Taine turned to them. "You're going to have to get used to it because Heko has slept with her sword since she was six."

"That's just an expression," Heko said.

Muffled shouts sounded, and rapid footfalls ran past the tent. Taine looked back outside. "Something's going on."

The others went to the tent's opening. Soldiers were being roused and ordered to the mess tent. Melie, with a worried expression, strode toward their tent.

"The Kuntians have taken Balderon," she said.

Zandar gasped, and her hands flew to her mouth.

"Taken," Heko said.

"Like they took Artocia, to stop a muster of troops to help Ynit," Melie said.

"So Balderon is occupied." Heko rubbed her chin and stared at the bluff across the hollow. "What are you going to do?"

"We're going to loosen that hold in the north," Melie said. "Balderon is too close to the Northern Territories for it to remain occupied."

Heko ran her hand through her hair. "Uh, maybe we can help."

"We?"

"Emoria," Heko said.

"Exactly what do you have in mind?" Melie asked.

"You don't have a large reserve here," Heko said. "We could supplement it."

"Supplement," Melie said.

"I think I have a plan that could work," Heko said.

"I'm certainly open to hearing any plan," Melie said.

Taine touched Heko's arm. "Are you thinking of going to Emoria?"

Heko nodded. "From here it's just as easy to get to."

Zandar's eyes widened. "We're going to Emoria?"

"Yes," Heko said. "Whether the commander and I agree on a plan or not. It's the only place we can go at the moment without worrying about that army."

"We're going to Emoria?" Zandar sucked in her breath. "Do you think my family's all right?"

"If it's like Artocia," Heko said, "they're fine. The Kuntians aren't interested in fighting or any kind of conflict if they can help it. Besides, even if we got into Balderon we couldn't help get rid of the

Kuntians. But we have a chance if we go to Emoria and officially get involved."

"Emoria." Zandar couldn't keep the wonder out of her voice.

Heko laughed. "Let's see what we can do to help with this little problem."

"WISH WE HAD borrowed one of those tents." Nohi pulled the saddle off her horse and ducked under the shallow shelter bluff. The late afternoon sky billowed with black storm-filled clouds. The wind whipped and howled across the top of the hollow in the foothills of the Phytian Mountains but they were deep enough to be mostly protected from it.

"Don't let any warrior in Emoria hear you say something like that," Taine said as she led the horses into a larger shelter bluff across the narrow hollow.

"You don't want to know what they'd do to you." Heko piled the saddles and their gear as deep under the shelter as possible and then looked out and up at the sky. She glanced around and saw a tree that had finally given in to erosion and had toppled over. "Let's get some branches from that tree and lay them over the opening here. That should keep most of the rain and wind out."

"You just want to make it more comfortable for Zandar," Taine said.

Heko turned to her and straightened. "She's not a warrior or a scout."

Zandar looked up from pushing stones into a fire circle. The blackened roof and stones on the floor were evidence that the shelter was a popular place to camp. "And I appreciate it. Last night was the first time I didn't sleep in a bed, and I've never slept outside." Thunder rumbled in the distance. "In a storm."

"These warriors may talk tough but they want to be sheltered away from the storm as much as anyone," Taine said.

"Says the scout, who boasts they can sleep in any weather anywhere," Heko said.

"But not if there are more comfortable choices," Taine said.

The thunder rumbled closer.

"Come on. Let's get those branches." Heko sprinted down the edge of the bluff, followed by the others.

They piled enough branches to give them a good shelter and got a small fire going.

Heko's nostril's twitched, and she peered outside at the sound of large raindrops splattering against the soft sand, followed by the steady clatter of rain.

"The evening meal has to be whatever we have left from the camp." Nohi pulled out several rough cloth bundles from a saddlebag, unwrapped them, and spread them out on a flat rock. "Help yourself."

They grabbed hunks of white cheese and bread and ate in surprisingly good humor.

"Two of us have never been to Emoria," Nohi said. "Are there things we should know about. So we don't commit some grievous error that may lead to unending teasing?"

Heko and Taine looked at each other and laughed.

"Everyone's going to wonder why we couldn't have found life companions in Emoria," Taine said. "The number of broken hearts as far as Heko is concerned is certainly in the hundreds."

Heko sighed and shook her head. "You always had a trail of girls following after you."

Nohi held up her hands. "I heard the both of you are considered the most roguishly attractive Emorans who ever lived, and you've both broken your share of hearts. That's why you came to Balderon after all, to get away from all that adoration."

Zandar and Nohi laughed. Heko knew she looked just as sheepish Taine.

"But seriously, it's not every day strangers enter Emoria, especially strangers not of Emoran blood," Nohi said.

"We should be riding into Emor about mid-afternoon," Heko said. "By that time the outer guards will have alerted the city we're in Emoria, and everyone will forget their work and their training and whatever else they're doing and casually watch the square or find some excuse to be there."

Taine doubled over with laughter. "That's so true."

"But all we have to do is ignore them and go straight to the palace," Heko said. "I can guarantee Taine's mothers will be there, waiting with my mothers."

"Planning our joinings and swapping all those embarrassing stories of us growing up," Taine said.

"Hyek will give orders to the kitchens to prepare my favorite foods," Heko said, "and we'll have our evening meal in her private chambers."

Taine snorted her laughter. "She'll find a chamber for Zandar as far away from Heko's as possible and still be in Emor."

"And your mothers will put Nohi up in the warrior's camp," Heko said.

"In other words," Zandar said, "Nohi and I just have to be ourselves."

Heko grinned. "Everyone will love both of you."

# Chapter 18

THEY RODE BETWEEN several large boulders into a stand of tall thin trees. The atmosphere changed to a stillness before a storm.

Zandar looked around in curiosity. "Are we in Emoria?"

Several masked warriors stepped out from behind trees in answer. Zandar's eyes widened as she turned to Heko.

Heko grinned, dismounted, and gave her reins to Taine. She then helped Zandar, who was not used to being on a horse, to dismount and had to fight from wrapping her arms around her. Maybe coming to Emoria wasn't such a good idea. She'd have to be on her guard every heartbeat not to show too much affection. How, in Laur's name, did this tradition ever get started?

"I'll have to be the tough stoic warrior now, I guess," she whispered.

"I understand because I know what's in your heart," Zandar replied in a low voice. "Now tell me why all those warriors are standing in the trees with masks on and looking very menacing."

"They want you and Nohi to surrender your swords."

Taine and Nohi dismounted behind them and waited.

A warrior strode onto the trail and stood in front of them. At a silent command, all the warriors unsheathed their swords and pressed the flat of the blades to their foreheads in a salute.

"Welcome home, my princess," the warrior said.

"Good to be home, Iren," Heko said. "This is my cousin, Nohi, from Balderon. This is Zandar Reevler also of Balderon. She was caught in an occupation by an invading army. In order to rescue her I made her an Emoran citizen under the limitations of our laws."

Iren nodded. "We'll take your horses to the stables."

"Thank you," Heko said.

Iren looked back, and four warriors approached and took the horses' reins. Heko watched them give Zandar as curious a look as she was giving them. She hoped they accepted her without question.

Zandar watched as the warriors led the horses off the trail and disappeared into the trees. "I would have gladly given up this sword, considering it's for show anyway."

Taine and Nohi grinned as Heko exchanged looks with them.

"The sword is yours." Heko shifted and scuffed the toe of her boot into the dirt.

"She bought it from my mother before we left," Nohi said. "It's a beautiful ceremonial sword. When my mother wheedled out of Heko why she wanted to buy it, she tried to give it as a gift."

"But Heko piled the silver on the counter," Taine said.

Nohi grinned. "Expect a nice joining gift from my mother. She really wants to welcome you to the family."

Heko shook her head and started up the trail. Zandar joined her, and Nohi and Taine followed behind.

"Thank you for the sword," Zandar said. "I'll cherish it, along with this." She pulled the black-and-purple sash from her belt pouch. "I always carry it with me. I understood what Taine was saying when she told me you won it for me."

"Taine overstepped the boundaries of courtship," Heko said.

Zandar smiled. "I know, but I'm glad she did."

Heko wrapped her arm around Zandar. "Me, too."

"Aren't all the hidden sentries and curious Emorans trying to catch a glimpse of the stranger going to tease you?" Zandar asked.

"I want to make sure they know exactly who the stranger is," Heko said, "and they can't tease if they don't show themselves."

Zandar looked amused. "The rules of teasing are quite complex. Why are we walking into the city instead of riding?"

"We're entering from the southwest side," Heko said. "The only way in is on foot through a narrow cave. The stables are on top of the northeast bluff, so the horses have to be taken around the city."

"I'm trying to picture a city tucked up here but I can't," Zandar said.

"It's like no other city." Heko couldn't keep the pride out of her voice.

"I guess I'll be seeing it soon enough," Zandar said.

"Very soon."

"What did you mean about the limitations of your law?" Zandar asked. "About these papers I carry."

Heko sighed. "Those papers are legal but not permanent. The queen still has to issue official papers."

Zandar gave Heko a playful look. "At least I get to wear the sword. Why did they want to take away Nohi's and mine sword anyway?"

"Only citizens can carry weapons in Emoria," Heko said.

"Interesting." Zandar nodded and then stared as the woods opened onto a narrow hollow with a creek burbling down the middle. A waterfall plummeted into a clear pool at the horseshoe-shaped end of the hollow.

Heko led the way on the rocky path alongside the creek. Near the waterfall, large boulders stood in their way. Before they walked between the two halves of a towering boulder, she whacked the rock a few times and then looked up the way they were to go. Satisfied, she led them through a maze of fissures and streets, created by large boulders split by falling and weathering. She occasionally thumped the rock before entering a new section.

"Why do you keep hitting the rock?" Zandar asked.

Heko gave her an amused look. "Snakes."

Zandar's eyebrows shot up. "Snakes?"

"They like to lounge in the afternoon sun on top of the boulders," Heko said. "If they're going to fall, it's better if they do it when we're not walking beneath them."

Zandar looked up. "I kind of like snakes."

"They're much nicer when they're not falling on you without warning." Heko stopped at an opening in the bluff wall. The cavern glowed orange from lanterns inset in the walls.

"They lit the way for us," Taine said. "Nice to be in the company of the princess."

Zandar shrugged. "I think it's nice."

"That's good because you're going to feel like everyone in Emoria is watching every move you make," Taine said. "Which they will be."

Zandar grinned. "I won't mind as long as Heko is also watching."

"She's good," Heko said.

Taine laughed and walked ahead of them into the cave. "Come on, Nohi. Let's go entertain everyone."

A grinning Nohi walked past Heko and Zandar into the cave.

Taine and Nohi disappeared around a curve, and Heko pulled Zandar into her arms and gave her a quick kiss. "I don't know when I'll be able to do that again."

"Hmmm. I have the feeling you know a lot of private places where we just happen to find ourselves," Zandar said.

Heko buried her face on Zandar's shoulder and shook with

laughter. She lifted her head and kissed Zandar's cheek. "Please. Don't ever change."

"I don't plan to." Zandar looked into the cave. "I suppose Taine and Nohi are wondering why we're not following them."

"They know why we're not following them." Heko took Zandar's hand and pulled her into the cave.

After several curves the other opening of the cave almost blinded them with the intense afternoon sun reflecting on the barely visible white stone outside.

"Welcome to the city of Emor," Heko said as she stepped into the light and turned to Zandar.

Zandar walked out of the cave and after blinking away the brightness of the sun, stared in stunned wonder at the city carved into bluffs of white stone. Murals of Emoran warriors towered over the square which was filled with . . . Emorans. Bold young warriors and shy acolytes in violet. Emorans holding babies. Little Emorans caught up in the excitement and running to them for a closer look. Older and elderly Emorans. A whole world rarely seen by an outsider.

They all watched with a respectful curiosity.

"Taine and Nohi are already at the palace." Heko smiled at Zandar's stunned expression. "You're going to help me rule this city and country someday."

Zandar's attention snapped to Heko. "I hope you don't mind if I find that idea incredibly daunting."

"You'll get used to this place quick enough," Heko said. "Come on. I want you to meet my mothers."

The gathered woman parted as they walked across the square. Heko nodded greetings, and was amused when their attention quickly shifted to Zandar. She was happy to see mostly curiosity. She was quite sure no one had really fallen in love with her. Laur was more benevolent than that.

She was not surprised to see the palace doors wide open and the Elders Council in a semicircle behind Hyek and Niko. Her mothers were doing their best to look like they were waiting patiently but Heko knew they'd be rushing to them if they didn't have to maintain a royal dignity.

Near the palace doors, Taine's mothers looked like they were doing their best to embarrass both Taine and Nohi. Heko thanked Laur she and Zandar would be spared such public humiliation. There were some advantages to being a princess.

She turned to Zandar and took her hand. Zandar raised an eyebrow. "Don't worry, I'm following tradition. I'm officially presenting my future life companion to my mothers. I won't be teased."

They approached Hyek and Niko, who both smiled in anticipation.

"Zandar, I'd like you to meet my mothers, Niko, Nohi's aunt, and Hyek, queen of Emoria." She gazed at her mothers. "I'd like to meet Zandar Reevler of Balderon."

"Well met, Zandar," Niko said.

Hyek stepped forward and took Zandar's hand. "Welcome to Emoria, Zandar."

"Thank you." Zandar looked a bit overwhelmed and in awe. "I'm happy to be here."

Hyek released Zandar's hand and put it back into Heko's, who beamed at Zandar. "And I'm sure one of you will explain why you're touring the countryside just as we're getting word the Kuntians are invading the Southern Territories."

"The roads don't have as many people on them." Heko gave her best innocent look. "And you can get a table in the taverns."

Hyek sighed and pulled Heko into a hug. "I'm glad to see you're well."

Niko took her turn to embrace Heko and then held her at arm's length. "Maybe not quite well, but much better."

"You all look like you've been on quite an adventure," Hyek said. "We've prepared rooms for Zandar and Nohi in the palace."

Taine approached them with her mothers in tow. "Zandar. I'd like you to meet my mothers, Tera and Eorgis."

Zandar smiled at the pair of women. "I'm happy to meet you."

"I look forward to hearing about what brought you here," Tera said.

Hyek turned to Heko. "As we all are."


ZANDAR'S MIND KEPT wandering from Taine's recounting of her rescue and how they ended up in Emoria. She had never imagined such an intimate eating chamber or one so unique. The chamber was round with an equally round table cut away in the middle so the servers could enter the chamber and deliver food to each person.

She was fascinated by the pride on the faces of Taine's mothers. She was curious about how Niko watched Heko with open affection tinged with concern, and Hyek maintained a more warrior reserve. She then remembered Niko grew up in Balderon and, obviously, was not a warrior.

"And that's how we're here instead of in Balderon," Taine concluded.

Hyek put down her mug and reached across the table past Niko and laid a hand on Zandar's arm. "Maybe you'll be more successful than we've been in tempering Heko's impulsive heroics."

"I admit I was extremely happy to see her when she appeared at my door in Artocia," Zandar said. "But, even though she begged me not to feel guilty, I can't help but feel guilty about her getting beat up."

Hyek squeezed her arm. "It's a badge of honor for her. We'll just have to make sure she takes care of herself a bit until she's completely healed."

Zandar smiled and turned to Heko. "It'll be my pleasure."

Heko gazed as if mesmerized at her.

"Heko's gotten too relaxed in Balderon," Taine said. "The untraditional courtship technique, and no one around to tease her."

Eorgis gave her daughter an amused look. "What about you and Nohi and everyone in the safe house?"

Taine shifted and glanced at Nohi. "Uh, because we were in Balderon, and things are different there, we kind of called a truce on teasing each other. And none of the others ever saw Heko and Zandar together."

"Ah." Eorgis nodded. "So Heko's not the only one who got a little too relaxed in Balderon. And did the others tease you and Nohi?"

Taine sighed. "Some."

The four mothers laughed.

"We have a lot to talk about tomorrow," Hyek said. "I suggest that all of you get some rest. You look as exhausted as you probably are."

Heko stood and pulled Zandar up with her then released her hand. Taine and Nohi grinned and stood up, too.

Hyek gave them a sympathetic look. "I wish we were planning a pair of joinings tomorrow. You know how uncomfortable I am with long waits." She sighed. "But I wouldn't deprive your families of seeing you joined."

"When this trouble with the Kuntians is taken care of," Heko said, "we'll be joined."

"IT'S NOT FAIR Zandar gets to stay in the room next to you, and Nohi doesn't get to stay in my house." Taine crossed her arms as they paused in the outer gallery of the palace.

"My mothers know everyone in the palace is watching us," Heko said. "They're, uh, also worried about my lungs. They want us to leave our doors open so Zandar can hear if I have a coughing fit or something."

"That's one thing I don't understand," Zandar said. "Why don't you just post one of these guards outside your door?"

"Uh . . ." Heko looked down at her feet.

"Because you and Heko are going to be joined," Taine said. "Another woman would not feel it was her place to take care of her."

"I guess it'll take a while to learn the nuances of your society," Zandar said.

"That still doesn't stop me from walking you to your chamber," Taine said to Nohi.

Heko laughed. "Just don't linger there too long. We're back in Emoria. Stories spread as fast as the wind, and you know the warriors will take any excuse to challenge Nohi."

"Challenge?" Nohi asked.

"They may restrain themselves since you're my cousin," Heko said. "But that also might be a reason for them to want to make a challenge."

"Don't even tease me about this," Nohi said.

Heko laughed. "I don't want you to get a big head but you're as good as most of the warriors here."

"I don't care," Nohi said. "I'd rather not add that to everything else."

"They're going to be more interested in going to war than seeing if you're good enough for Taine," Heko said.

Taine looked as if she wasn't sure whether to be insulted or not.

"Rumor has it our princess has returned," said a voice behind them. "But all I see is a pale counterfeit sagging under the weight of lovesickness."

They turned around as Tarna, a blonde-haired warrior, sauntered up to them.

"Although, I've heard the paleness is from injuries." Tarna stopped and crossed her arms.

"You heard right," Heko said. "I see you got your braid."

"All of us did," Tarna said. "We weren't going to let you have all the fun." She raked her eyes over Zandar.

"This is Zandar," Heko said. "Zandar, meet Tarna."

"Well met, Zandar." Tarna bowed her head.

"Well met, Tarna," Zandar said.

"I hear you didn't know Heko was a princess until after you came to an understanding with her," Tarna said.

"I thought she was just a warrior making some extra money as an Auxiliary Guard," Zandar said.

Tarna's gaze shifted to Zandar's shoulder. "At least enough to afford that sword you're wearing."

Taine snorted a laugh. "Heko would have paid anything for that sword."

Heko shot Taine a look and then returned her attention to Tarna, who wore an amused expression. "Lots of nice things you can do with a sword."

Heko raised an eyebrow. "Looks like I'll find out before you do."

Tarna straightened, and a hint of discomfort flickered over her face. "I always thought you'd go for a scout or maybe a warrior."

"I got the next best thing." Heko grinned. "Zandar's a military historian."

Tarna gave Zandar a puzzled look. "Military historian?"

"She knows about every battle ever fought," Heko said. "Every weapon ever used. Everything."

"Really." Envy flashed across Tarna's face and a hint of sadness. "It'll be interesting having a military historian around." She bit her lip. "I need to get back to the camp."

Heko watched as Tarna strode down the corridor and into the foyer. "I had no idea."

"Uh." Taine looked at the floor.

"You knew?" Heko asked.

"I think it was just a crush," Taine said. "We left before she had a chance to get over it."

Heko bit her lip. "I hope so."

Taine clasped Heko's shoulder. "You look like you're about ready to fall over. Get some sleep. Things will be clearer in the morning."

Heko nodded and turned to Zandar. "Think you can find the way?"

Zandar laughed. "Not after going there once. This place is a maze."

"You'll get used to it," Heko said.

Zandar grinned. "Why do I get the feeling I'm going to hear that a lot?"

# Chapter 19

NIKO STOOD IN the doorway of Heko's chamber and watched her daughter sleep. Not the light sleep of a warrior, but a heavy exhausted sleep, even after a night's rest.

She sighed and went to the next opened doorway and gently rapped on the door.

Zandar was dressed in her own clothes and brushing out her hair. She looked up and smiled. "Good morning. Come in."

Niko entered the chamber. "I've asked Orla, the tailor, to come and fit you with your own set of leathers."

"You don't . . . I mean . . ." Zandar emitted an embarrassed laugh. "Sorry. I haven't quite gotten used to the idea Emoria is going to be my home. To tell you the truth, I wasn't thinking past wanting to let Heko know I was interested. I knew that meant loving her enough to want to be joined to her but the whole idea of Emoria was still an abstraction."

"I understand," Niko said. "Remember, I grew up in Balderon. Even as an Emoran, I always felt Emoria was half buried in dreams."

Zandar put down her brush and stretched out the kinks in her back. "It's still buried in half dreams for me. The only thing that is truly real is Heko." She gave Niko a sheepish look. "I keep forgetting she's a princess. To me she's the shy, sweet warrior who never looked bored when I talked to her for sandmarks on the coach to and from Artocia and when we walked around the festival. I found myself looking forward to her company, and then I couldn't stop thinking about her."

Niko gave her an amused look. "I hear you can't figure out why everyone stares at her."

Zandar laughed. "The first time I witnessed it was at the festival. It's not that I think she's ugly. I think she's cute in a sweet kind of way. But I don't see what everyone else seems to see."

"You have no idea how perfect you are for her," Niko said. "Which brings me to why I'm here. The guard reported Heko had three coughing fits and wheezed through most of the night."

Zandar sighed. "Yeah. I had to go in there three times to make sure she was all right."

"And the fits eased right away," Niko said.

Zandar cocked her head. "Yes."

"And she didn't cough or wheeze at all the two nights you were traveling," Niko said.

"No." Zandar drew the word out.

"But she did wheeze the night in the safe house." Niko almost laughed at Zandar's expression. "I had a chat with Taine this morning. She and Nohi made sure you slept next to Heko because of a power of healing Laur blesses couples with. They weren't sure if it worked with someone who isn't Emoran but gave it a try anyway."

"Why didn't they just come out and tell me about it instead of all the warrior posturing?" Zandar asked.

Niko chuckled. "You answered your own question. The posturing sometimes hides their fear and uncertainty."

Zandar nodded. "Taine got upset when Heko had the coughing fit in the military camp. I had the feeling she could never vent her frustration like that here."

"Heko's lucky to have found an outsider who understands our ways," Niko said.

"The more I learn, the more I realize how much I don't know or understand," Zandar said.

"But you understand us on an important basic level," Niko said. "And you understand how to behave around a warrior partner." She sighed. "We all know Heko is going to want to lead the army that rids Balderon of the Kuntians, and we won't be able to stop her. We would never insult a warrior's honor like that. If you were an Emoran you would be getting joined as soon as we could make preparations. She needs your strength to get well before she rides into battle."

Zandar grinned. "But I am an Emoran—at least temporarily."

"How old are you?" Niko asked.

"Nineteen," Zandar said.

"Underage in Balderon," Niko said.

"But of legal age in Emoria," Zandar said.

"Tell me the truth," Niko said. "How would your mother react if we sent her word you've been joined to Heko?"

Zandar bit her lip, walked a circle, and then stopped and faced Niko. "Tell her the whole story. If you want, I'll write it. She'll not only understand, she'll love it. She'll be disappointed she won't be present at the joining but the story she'll be able to tell her friends will more than make up for it."

"Since we've just sent word to the Federation Council that we have sided with the Southern Territories in this conflict, we are now in a state of war." Niko gave Zandar a thoughtful look. "That means you can be joined in what we call a Temple ceremony and then have the full ceremony after the war is over."

"That's even better," Zandar said. "She'll have this great story to tell and get to witness an Emoran joining. She's spent her life lamenting the fact I don't want to be a merchant. She could never grasp the idea that I'd be happy living off of a scholar's wage to do what I love to do. This joining will put her mind at ease."

"What if Heko really was an ordinary warrior?" Niko asked.

"I thought she was just a warrior when I let her know I was interested," Zandar said. "I was prepared to defy my mother, if she had a problem with my choice of life companion. But she really likes Heko, and even though she would have had concerns about how we'd live on the combined wages of a scholar and warrior, she would have been pleased to have Heko a part of her family."

"What about the merchant your mother wants you to be joined with?" Niko asked.

Zandar laughed. "You've been talking to Taine and Nohi. Brandle, the merchant in question, was responsible for Heko's beating. My mother wrote and told me the ruffians involved confessed she had paid them to attack Heko. Brandle had convinced the authorities they'd risk trouble with Emoria if word got out that the beating was something other than the work of street ruffians. So no one outside a small circle of merchants knows of Brandle's involvement."

"You know you're going to have to tell Heko," Niko said.

"I know." Zandar smiled. "I think she'll be more reasonable about it than Taine or Nohi."

Niko's eyes sparkled. "I think you're right." She gave Zandar an affectionate look. "Hyek and I are so pleased and delighted with you. And Heko is completely smitten."

Zandar looked down at the floor. "I'm smitten with her, too." She raised her head. "But it's going to take a while to get used to her as a princess. I kind of like that shy, sweet warrior."

"And that's who she'll always be to you," Niko said. "Trust me on this. I speak from experience. Now let's go see how Heko is doing."

Zandar grinned and followed Niko into the corridor and to Heko's room.

Niko stopped in the doorway. "Still asleep. Heko's never needed much sleep, so it's very unusual for her to be so exhausted."

Zandar took a deep breath. "I'm not feeling guilty. I'm not feeling guilty."

"Actually, it's Brandle's fault," Niko said. "You said so yourself. Heko would have dishonored her no matter who sponsored her in the competition. She challenged Heko. Heko took the challenge. Only Brandle is to blame for this."

"But she wouldn't even have paid attention to Heko if she wasn't pursuing me and noticed I was more interested in Heko," Zandar said.

"There's one thing you'll have to learn about living around warriors," Niko said. "They get challenged and they fight and they get hurt. They often get challenged to see if they're worthy of a cousin or a sister or a friend."

Zandar nodded. "It'll take me a while to adjust to that."

"Why don't you go wake her." Niko nodded at Heko.

Zandar flashed her a quizzical look and then walked across the chamber to the bed against the far wall. She looked down at Heko, relaxed in sleep, and gently shook her shoulder.

Heko groaned and opened her eyes as she slowly rolled onto her back. She blinked and then smiled at Zandar.

"Your mother thought it was time to wake you," Zandar said.

Heko frowned and then looked toward the door. Niko walked into the chamber to stand next to Zandar.

"We need you to help us convince Hyek to let you be joined today," Niko said.

"What?" Heko sat up.

Niko laughed. "Get dressed. Then we'll explain it to you."

HYEK STARED OUT the window of her study and watched her people go about their everyday lives in the square below. She had just committed Emoria's resources to ridding the Southern Territories of the Kuntians. Now her life companion, daughter, and her daughter's soon-to-be life companion were determined to use that decision to their advantage.

It's not that she didn't want Heko joined as soon as possible. Niko was convinced Zandar was blessed with the power to help Heko heal. But she was worried about Zandar's mother reaction to her daughter being joined because circumstances allowed her to be made an Emoran citizen and consequently of legal age.

She turned around. "It seems I'm going to have to trust your word you know your mother well enough that she'll accept your joining in the proper spirit."

"I know and understand my mother," Zandar said. "She'll be fine with this, and she'll enjoy the notoriety. She can't help it, she's a merchant. And she likes Heko."

Hyek turned to her daughter who stood next to Zandar looking a bit dazed about the sudden discussions of an immediate joining. "She did take Heko in and paid for the healer, even after she was moved back to the safe house."

"I didn't know that," Heko said.

Hyek approached Heko and put a hand on her shoulder. "Are you ready to be joined?"

Heko met Zandar's eyes and grinned. "Yes."

Hyek squeezed Heko's shoulder and then took Zandar's hand into both of hers. "Normally, I'd be apprehensive about letting an outsider into our society. But your scholarship and interest in warriors and your understanding of Emoran society puts my mind at ease. Are you ready to be joined?"

"Yes." Zandar looked at Heko and smiled.

"Then I'd better let Keine know." Hyek released Zandar's hand. "She'll be delighted to find out she gets to oversee a joining today."


HEKO SAT ON the stone bench in the small Temple chamber, spinning her dagger, using her fingers as an axis.

"Zandar wouldn't be very happy if you got joined with your boot sliced open and your toes cut off." Taine leaned a shoulder on the doorjamb.

Heko stopped the dagger and looked up. "Just thinking."

Taine walked into the chamber and sat on a bench against the wall adjacent to Heko. "I know it's not second thoughts, so what could you be thinking so deeply about?"

"I was just thinking how amazing this is," Heko said. "That Zandar and I are about to be joined. She's such a miracle I can't believe she's real and she really loves me."

Taine slumped against the wall. "I think everyone has thoughts like that. Like I still can't understand why Nohi fell for me."

Heko nodded and sheathed her dagger. "I think warriors and scouts are naturally insecure about these things. I wish you and Nohi were getting joined today."

Taine gave her a rueful grin. "Unlike Zandar's mother, Nohi's mother would never forgive us."

Heko chuckled and looked up at the acolyte in the doorway.

"Keine is ready." The acolyte seemed to struggle to be solemn and couldn't keep her excitement and delight from her face.

"Thank you, Sian," Heko said. She and Taine stood and smoothed down their leathers and straightened their braids.

They followed Sian to the main chamber. Waterfalls plummeted into shallow pools. Nohi and Zandar walked out of another chamber at the same time, and Heko stopped and stared at Zandar in her tailored leathers and carrying the sword on her back as if she was born to it.

Zandar turned, and her smile almost buckled Heko's knees.

Taine nudged her, and they walked to the center of the chamber where Hyek and Niko waited with Keine, the High Follower of Laur.

Heko and Zandar stood next to each other in front of Hyek. Taine and Nohi, exchanging amused glances, took their places behind them.

Hyek unsheathed her sword and lowered it, flat side up, between Heko and Zandar until it pointed at the far wall.

"Hekolatis Ketlas, princess of Emoria, and Zandar Reevler of Balderon are here before Laur to be joined," Hyek said. "They are here to declare their lifelong pledge to each other."

Hyek nodded, and Heko and Zandar faced each other.

Heko pulled a wrist bracer of woven leather from her belt pouch and held it up. "I give my life to be with Zandar Reevler for as long as I walk this earth and until Laur's waters stop flowing."

Zandar pulled an identical wrist bracer from her belt pouch. "I give my life to be with Hekolatis Ketlas for as long as I walk this earth and until Laur's waters stop flowing."

Over the sword, Heko slipped the bracer onto Zandar's wrist and Zandar, in turn, covered Heko's wrist with her bracer. Heko ran her finger over the edge of the blade and held up her hand. Zandar mirrored the action and showed no discomfort as the cold blade slit her skin. They pressed their hands together and their blood mingled.

"Let it be written that citizens of Emoria have witnessed the joining of Hekolatis and Zandar." Hyek dropped the sword out of the way and took a step back.

Their hands still clasped together, Heko shyly leaned forward and gave Zandar a gentle kiss.

The temple bells in the tower far above them tolled and cheering echoed through the city.

"So much for a quiet, private ceremony," Hyek said.

A grinning Taine stepped forward and gave Heko and Zandar rags to wipe the blood off of their hands. "The citizens only agreed to this joining because you promised them one befitting a princess followed by three days of celebrating once the war is over."

"And a joining and a celebration they'll get." Niko pulled Zandar into a hug. "Welcome to the family."

"It's like a wonderful dream," Zandar said.

Heko took her hand. "Allow me the honor of presenting you to Emoria." She led Zandar to the doors of the Temple. A pair of giddy acolytes opened the doors for them.

They stepped outside and were stopped by a wall of cheering coming from hundreds of women in the square and just as many on the paths that switched-backed up the bluff walls. Heko held up Zandar's hand, and the noise grew so loud the echoes were probably heard all the way to Balderon.

Heko gave Zandar a delighted grin and leaned close to her ear. "They love you and so do I."

Zandar turned to Heko. "I love you, too," she said in Heko's ear.

"Heko! Zandar!" the citizens of Emoria chanted.

Heko realized that her restless soul finally felt at peace. All it took was the perfect woman.

# Chapter 20

"THIS LINE OF hills can keep our approach hidden until we are within striking distance of Balderon." Nohi ran her fingers across the map spread out on a table in the palace war room.

"Those hills were used to the advantage of the Southern Territories army during the Twenty-Year War," Zandar said. "As long as the Kuntians think Emoria is neutral they won't look east for a threat and they have their eye on the army—except Melie's hidden troops."

Pyam crossed her arms and studied the terrain around Balderon. "What about having the main force come from the north. From here." She put her finger on a range of hills northeast of the city. "They wouldn't expect a northern assault."

"And the terrain to the north is rough enough we could get close before being seen," Nohi said.

"The main advanced guard of the Ynitian Regulars were able to get into position within fifteen or twenty paces of the north gate at night," Zandar said.

"We can only hope the Kuntians don't know their military history," Pyam said.

"We don't want to have all our battles in the streets." Heko stared at the map of the city. "What's this?" She put her finger on a spot near the north wall.

Nohi and Zandar leaned over the map.

"Isn't that the old waste tunnel?" Nohi asked.

"It must be because the new one is here." Zandar pointed to a place on the west wall.

Heko rubbed her chin and stared at the map. "Is it still intact?"

Nohi shrugged.

"I don't know," Zandar said.

"We can send scouts in," Jygar said. "Do we have a structural map of Balderon?"

Hyek turned to a guard. "Tell Tesle we need maps of Balderon showing the structure of the city."

The guard nodded and disappeared down the long corridor.

"What about . . . ?" Heko couldn't suck in a breath.

Zandar and Taine grabbed her before she slumped to the floor.

Heko pulled in a breath with audible relief. She slowly straightened and cleared her lungs with a coughing fit.

Hyek's eyes were wide with concern as she rushed to Heko and put a hand on her cheek. "Laur's waterfalls. If you hadn't convinced me about the joining, I would have insisted on it now."

"How do you expect to lead this campaign?" Jygar asked, alarmed.

"I will lead this campaign," Heko said.

"But . . ."

Heko stepped away from Zandar and Taine, and walked around the table to Jygar. "No argument."

They faced each other for several tense heartbeats.

Jygar finally lowered her eyes. "I think you've demonstrated you're strong enough to lead us."

"There's more to leading an army than being able to swing a sword," Heko said.

"I just fear the warriors won't react well if they see any physical weakness from you," Jygar said. "It's your own fault for never being ill or injured. We're used to seeing you strong and healthy."

Heko put a hand on Jygar's shoulder. "I know. They'll get used to it. They have to. I'm only human after all."

"A human with a special blessing from Laur," Jygar said. "It's late, and you're as pale as the moon. Let your life companion give you a healing sleep. We'll research the city and the terrain and come up with possible strategies for you to look at in the morning."

Zandar stepped up next to Heko and put her hand on her arm. "I'm rather pleased to say that my first duty as your life companion is to take you to bed."

The tension flowed out of the chamber, and everyone grinned.

Hyek nodded. "An important lesson a warrior learns is to listen to her partner."

Heko wrapped her arm around Zandar. "I'll have no problem with listening to her wise advice."

Hyek laughed. "Just try to get some rest tonight."

"Yeah, right," Taine said. "Come on, Nohi. Emoran tradition dictates that we accompany the newly joined couple to their door."

Nohi grinned. "It'll be my pleasure."

Heko turned to her mother. "Thank you for trusting Zandar and I have done the right thing. And thank you for letting us fight for the Southern Territories."

"Thank you for having the good sense to find Zandar," Hyek said.

Zandar looked at her boots as Heko beamed with pride.


HEKO SAT ON the edge of the bed, not happy she could barely keep her eyes open. Not the way she had pictured her joining night at all.

Zandar finished putting the few belongings she had brought with her from Artocia into the holes cut in the stone wall. She then walked to Heko and knelt in front of her.

"I take it there are some strong traditions tied to the joining night." Zandar took Heko's hands.

Heko looked up at her. "Laur blesses the couple that sleeps skin to skin on their joining night."

Zandar smiled. "Sounds like a nice kind of blessing."

"It'll be sweet torture," Heko said.

Zandar wrapped her arms around Heko and kissed her. "It'll be a sweet night's sleep."

Heko pulled Zandar close and put her lips to her ears. "I want to give you more than a sweet night's sleep."

Zandar closed her eyes. "Let's start with the skin to skin and see what happens from there."

"Good plan," Heko breathed against Zandar's cheek.

She released Zandar and stood, bringing Zandar up with her. She took Zandar's hand and they walked around the chamber, dousing the lamps, leaving the fire in the fireplace to bathe them in an orange glow.

Heko then led Zandar to the bed and pulled down the leather covering. She faced Zandar and kissed her. "You have a bit of an advantage over me by growing up in a more open society. No Emoran sees another woman out of her leathers, so to speak, until their joining night." She gave Zandar a sheepish grin. "It's something we really look forward to."

Zandar grinned. "I admit that I've seen women in various states of undress. But I've never seen one I loved, never had one in my bed. So the way I see it, we're on pretty even ground here."

"So what strategy would you recommend?" Heko breathed against Zandar's cheek.

"I recommend a direct assault."

Heko pulled back and laughed at Zandar's impish grin. "How did I get so lucky to find you?"

"I thought I was the lucky one." Zandar fingered the leather ties on Heko's tunic.

Heko slipped a long finger under Zandar's throat laces and loosened them. She then took hold of the bottom of the tunic and pulled it up over Zandar's head. Her breath caught at the expanse of skin bathed in the golden light from the fire.

Zandar lifted Heko's tunic up and over her head and ran her hands down Heko's muscled arms and then loosened the ties on Heko's leggings that usually clung to her legs but were loose enough to drop to the floor. She had lost too much weight during her convalescence.

Heko loosened the laces on Zandar's leggings. She captured her eyes and then knelt and pushed the leggings down and off Zandar's legs. Her senses overloaded as she ran her hands up Zandar's legs and pressed her lips against her stomach.

Zandar sucked in her breath and laced her fingers in Heko's hair.

Heko looked up. "I surrender my defenses to you. I worship at the altar of your beauty."

Zandar smiled and messed up Heko's hair. "You're beyond exhausted." She lifted Heko up and wrapped her arms around her neck.

Heko buried her face in Zandar's hair and knew she had arrived in a paradise that would last for the rest of her life.

"Don't fall asleep on me yet." Zandar moved Heko to the bed and help her lay down. She then stretched out next to her and pulled her into her arms.

Heko snaked her arms around Zandar and captured her lips in a deep kiss. She then gazed at Zandar through sleepy eyes. "I'm sorry."

"I don't see anything to be sorry about." Zandar snuggled close to Heko. "I get to spend the night in the strong naked arms of an Emoran warrior. What military historian would complain about that?"

Heko shook with silent laughter. "Don't ever change."

"I won't, my sweet warrior," Zandar whispered. "Now take as much strength from me as you need and heal."

HEKO OPENED HER eyes and was caught in Zandar's tender gaze.

Zandar smiled. "Good morning."

Heko flexed her arms and pulled Zandar to her and captured her lips. "Yep. I'd say it's good."

"You didn't cough or even wheeze all night," Zandar said.

"I was wrapped in the warmth of love."

Zandar pulled her head back to focus on Heko. "You're not even exhausted."

Heko grinned. "I say what I feel."

"You have a sweet tongue, warrior." Zandar kissed Heko's cheek. "Your secret's safe with me."

Heko pressed her lips against Zandar's ear. "I wish I could show you how sweet my tongue is."

Zandar's breath caught. "Uh, what are you doing tonight?"

"I have an important engagement. Here. In this bed. With a beautiful woman." Heko ran her lips over Zandar's ear.

Zandar brushed her lips against Heko's. "Do you think she'd mind if I joined you?"

Heko laughed. She pulled Zandar on top of her and got lost in endless kisses.

She considered ignoring the pounding on the door but she knew whoever it was would keep pounding until she answered. She sighed, and Zandar collapsed on her in mock resignation.

"Do you have a death wish?" Heko called out.

"Nohi'd be very unhappy if you killed me," Taine said through the door. "Especially before our joining night. You know we wouldn't disturb you unless it was important."

"All right," Heko said. "What's up?"

"Taler and Ange just arrived from Balderon," Taine said. "It seems the Emorans in the safe house did some snooping around and have some important information."

"Where are they at?"

"In the mess hall," Taine said.

"We'll meet you there."

Zandar's eyes sparkled with affection. "Remember. We have a date, in this bed, tonight."

"I have no fear of forgetting that." Heko pulled Zandar down for a long kiss and then rolled them both out of the bed.

ZANDAR GOT ANOTHER dizzying tour of the maze masquerading as a palace as Heko led her on the short cut to the mess hall. "I'm never going to learn this place."

Heko grinned. "You'll know it better than any of us. The mess is through there."

"I think it's interesting the palace has a mess hall," Zandar said as they walked through an opened archway.

"We're a warrior society." Heko scanned the half-filled hall. "Over there."

Zandar found it interesting the Emorans gave them curious glances but returned to their food and conversations. The quiet respect they had for their princess touched her heart.

They sat down next to Taine and Nohi. Jygar, Ques, and Pyam were also at the table.

"Welcome to Emoria," Heko said. "I wish you were here under more joyous circumstances."

"You don't know how happy we are to know all of you are here," Ange said. "Everyone's been worried." She turned to Zandar. "When the Kuntians overran the city, everyone learned what was going on down south—that they had taken over Artocia. We heard the parents of students at the university were pretty upset, so we told your mother you were being rescued."

Zandar let out a relieved breath. "Thank you. I can only imagine my family's worry."

"I don't think you have to worry about her not approving of your joining with Heko," Ange said. "She thinks Emorans are wonderful."

Zandar grinned. "If she didn't think so, I'd make sure she did."

"So what's the news from Balderon?" Heko asked.

"We actually came here to report what was going on there and to let the queen know you weren't in Balderon," Taler said. "But I guess she knows that."

"We have a map of where the Kuntians are quartered." Ange pushed several sheets of parchment to Heko. "We also have a map of their patrol patterns and stationary guards. Also noted is how often the guard is changed and which post the guards come from."

"Makes this military historian's heart go pitter patter," Zandar said as a server put plates of food in front of her and Heko.

Heko grinned. "This is going to be the most documented military campaign in history."

"I've got to have my fun, too," Zandar said.

"Are you sure you two were just joined yesterday?" Ques asked. "Whatever happened to the awkward getting to know each part?"

"Between Zandar's endless questions and teasing, that part kind of got forgotten," Nohi said.

"Not the way an Emoran would have behaved around Heko," Pyam said.

"I didn't know she was a princess," Zandar said.

"Not that it stopped you once you found out," Taine said.

"It was too late," Zandar said. "I already set my sights on Heko the warrior."

"I didn't have a chance," Heko said.

"Warriors never do." Pyam leaned across the table and patted Heko's arm.

"Where are the Balderon soldiers?" Heko asked.

"They're being held in the garrison jails," Taler said.

Heko took a sip of her tea, scooped a spoonful of porridge into her mouth, and munched for a few thoughtful moments. "The Kuntians are expecting an attack from the outside. They're not expecting someone to pull the same tactic they pulled—infiltrate and then attack from the inside."

The others at the table put down their forks and mugs and waited.

"I have no doubt Emoran warriors and scouts can enter Balderon and dance jigs in the street without the Kuntians seeing us," Heko said. "Once we're in, we come out of the shadows and tickle them until they drop their weapons."

Pyam, Ques, and Jygar sat back and studied Heko.

"An interesting strategy," Jygar said.

"It'll work," Heko said. "I saw enough of how the Kuntians occupied Artocia. They feel their only threat is the army of the Southern Territories and they don't think them that much of a threat."

"The warriors, scouts, and archers are waiting for their assignments," Pyam said. "Shall I have your army assemble in the west meadow?"

Heko smiled at the sparkle of humor in Pyam's eyes. "We'll be there in a sandmark, and tell them to bring their dancing shoes."

# Chapter 21

"OF ALL THE things I've imagined about your military camp, I never imagined anything like this." Zandar followed Heko through a building that sprawled in the branches of squat trees with thick sinewy trunks. The rooms fit the contours of the branches and placement of the trees, so she had to keep one eye on her feet because of steps going up and down. She had enjoyed watching the meeting Heko had with her commanders in a round chamber in the middle of the structure.

"This was built many generations ago," Heko said. "It's usually used by weapons masters to watch training and drills." She stopped in front of a large window and pulled Zandar next to her.

Zandar stared out the window with widening eyes. From their position at the top of a tree, they could see the whole of the western meadow, including the military camp and the ceremonial circle.

"It looks like the entire country is up here," Zandar said.

Heko watched the women surging up from the city to join the crowds already gathered on the edge of the reviewing grounds. "It's been a long time since Emoria has been in a war. They want to know what their loved ones will be doing."

"I think they also want to see their princess," Zandar said.

Heko rolled her eyes but grabbed Zandar's hand and squeezed it and held it a few heartbeats before releasing it.

"Hmmm. Wasn't that a dangerous move?" Zandar asked.

Heko leaned into Zandar's ear and kissed her cheek. "I'm a warrior. I always know where spies may be lurking." She casually straightened as Ques appeared around a tree trunk and stepped up to where they stood.

"Smooth move," Zandar said under her breath.

"The troops are ready, my princess," Ques said.

Zandar thought the formality interesting, considering just a short time earlier, Heko had been just Heko with the meeting of the commanders.

"Ready to see an Emoran army in its glory?" Heko asked.

Zandar laughed. "Do you even have to ask?"

"This will be one for the chroniclers," Ques said. "Never has an Emoran army been led into battle by an unblooded warrior."

"You can present a formal protest later," Heko said.

Ques crossed her arms. "And deny all those young pups out there the opportunity to fight under their adventurer princess?"

Heko sighed. "So stop complaining about my extreme youth and inexperience."

"You're the first Emoran to lead an army who had to get permission from her mother because you're underage," Ques said.

Zandar stifled a laugh.

"Try to keep that one out of the chronicles, please," Heko said.

"It'll only add to your legend." Ques strolled away before Heko could argue with her.

"Come on, let's go prepare for battle," Heko said.

They stepped on the outside landing and faced a meadow crowded with curious women.

"I don't think I've ever seen this many woman at one time," Zandar said.

Heko chuckled as they walked down steps that wound around a large squat tree trunk. They strolled onto the dusty review grounds, and the women moved to the edges, leaving the space from the camp proper. Heko and Zandar joined Hyek and Niko on a long bank of dirt. Jygar, Pyam and Ques stood in front of them.

Pyam stepped forward. She unsheathed her sword and whipped it into a salute. A mob of archers ran from the barracks and fell into several lines at the back of the reviewing grounds.

Ques mimicked Pyam's actions, and scouts ran in from all directions and formed lines in front of the archers.

Jygar took her place next to Ques and saluted Heko. Warriors strode in long lines and fell into place in front of the scouts and archers.

Jygar, Ques, and Pyam, still facing Heko and Zandar, pointed their swords to the ground. The troops unsheathed their swords and saluted. The three master warriors sheathed their swords and the troops echoed the action in unison.

Jygar stepped forward. "Your army is ready to receive your orders, my princess."

"Thank you, Jygar," Heko said.

She looked out at the troops. "It seems the Kuntians have invaded the Southern Territories again. I guess they like getting beat."

The army chuckled and shifted a bit.

"We're in the perfect position to help remove these unwanted guests from Balderon," Heko said. "So that's what we're going to do. I've grown rather fond of the place and its people. Many Emorans have made Balderon their home and have lived a good life there." She looked at the women gathered around the army. "We're going to show the rest of the Southern Territories Emoria cares about its neighbors and has what it takes to help rid it of pesky nuisances like the Kuntians. These warriors, scouts, and archers standing before you comprise the best army in the world, and we are going to remind the world of that fact."

The women erupted in cheering. The army straightened and couldn't keep the proud expressions from their faces.

Heko turned her attention to her army. "Warriors, scouts, and archers. We'll gather in the valley meadow at six sandmarks tomorrow morning and take the northwest route to Balderon. Master Warrior Jygar, Master Scout Ques, and Master Archer Pyam will instruct you on what supplies to carry. Sleep well tonight, we'll be riding for two long days."

Heko scanned the eager faces riveted on her with an enigmatic expression. Zandar couldn't wait to ask her what she was feeling at that moment. Something for the chronicles for sure.

Heko straightened. "Master Warrior Jygar, Master Archer Pyam, and Master Scout Ques, dismiss your troops."


HEKO PROPPED UP on an elbow and watched Zandar sleep. She had felt Laur's blessing when they had made sweet love deep into the night. Her soul had soared even as her body became another sense, attuned to Zandar's body. She knew for the first time in her life, her body and soul were complete.

Zandar stirred, and her eyes fluttered open. She gave Heko a curious look. "You're awake."

"Yeah." Heko pulled her closer.

"You told your troops to get a good night's sleep," Zandar said. "You're as important as they are."

"Yeah." Heko nuzzled Zandar's cheek.

"You're changing the subject." Zandar chuckled.

"I know." Heko captured her lips. "Unfortunately, we have to get up soon."

Zandar sighed. "We really didn't get much sleep."

"No complaints here," Heko murmured in her ear.

"I'm certainly not complaining." Zandar tried to brush Heko's hair off her forehead. "You know, I'm going to spend the rest of my life doing that, and it's just going to fall back."

"I look forward to spending the rest of my life with you," Heko said.

"You know, everyone thinks Emorans are tough and emotionless," Zandar said. "But you're so wonderfully sweet and gentle. It's not . . . what I'm used to."

Heko frowned. "What do you mean?"

"The women I've been in contact with, merchants mostly, are, I don't know, pushy. They expect women to be interested in them and want what they want."

"Pushy."

Zandar kissed Heko's cheek. "Very unEmoran like."

"Was Brandle . . . pushy?"

Zandar smiled and smoothed out the hardened lines of Heko's face. "You're cute when you're indignant."

"I'm not indignant," Heko said. "I'm outraged. I'm glad I was able to rescue you away from such women."

"Even though it's the culture I grew up in, my studies of warrior societies, especially Emoria made me aware it wasn't the best for finding love and happiness," Zandar said. "I know I would have refused any arrangement with Brandle. My mother would have been disappointed but she would have never forced me against my will."

"I'm glad to hear that," Heko said. "I have to admit I wasn't happy with the idea of you being forced into an arranged joining."

Zandar wrapped her arms around Heko's neck. "Not happy? I'm sure you were ready to kill Brandle."

"I would have been pleased to have put her in her place if she had crossed the line with you," Heko said.

"I'm almost sorry I never got to see that," Zandar said.

A deep gong sounded and resounded five times.

Heko buried her head in Zandar's shoulder. "I guess the army isn't going to sneak away."

"It's not every day Emoria goes to war," Zandar said.

"When the war is over, we're going to an Inn away from everyone we know and spend a week in bed," Heko said.

Zandar grinned. "Only a week?"

Heko laughed. "You're so wonderful."


ZANDAR REALIZED HER jaw was constantly dropping but she couldn't help it. The valley outside the wall of Emor was lined with hundreds of women mingling with the deep shadows created by the orange glow of torches on the wall, in tall stone monuments scattered across the valley, and in sconces on the rocky bluffs themselves. The army was gathered in the middle, adjusting their equipment and mounts, and saying good-bye to loved ones.

Six palace guards approached Heko and Zandar.

"The queen is waiting for you on platform rock," one of the guards said.

Heko sighed, and they let the guards surround them and walk them to the flat elevated rock that stood in the middle of the valley near the tunnel opening Heko had run through what seemed like a lifetime ago.

Zandar's eyes widened at the formal-looking gathering on top of the stone. Hyek and Niko were in full Emoran leathers and armor surrounded by palace guards. "This is kind of a big event, I guess."

"Yeah," Heko said. "War is what we do best."

Their escort stopped at the bottom of the steps carved into the front of the rock.

"Time to be the center of attention," Heko said as they climbed the steps to the platform.

Niko lightly touched Zandar's arm. "Come stand next to me."

Heko blinked as Zandar took her place next to Niko and gave Hyek a confused look.

"Stand next to me," Hyek said.

Heko stood next to her and faced the wall of Emoria.

Hyek raised her hands. "Citizens of Emoria. Your attention for a few moments."

Zandar realized the natural acoustics of the canyon allowed Hyek's voice to be heard from the rock. The gathered citizens and army waited in silence for Hyek to continue.

"Our army is about to go into battle led by my daughter." Cheering arose. Hyek quieted them with her hands. "Since Heko will be coming of age away from Emoria, I wanted to make sure all of you who have watched her grow into a formidable warrior witness her receiving her braid."

The cheering was so loud it echoed around the canyon.

Heko stared at her, stunned.

The cheering died away.

Hyek pulled a braid from her belt pouch. "When Heko left Emoria she was a newly-braided warrior. In Balderon she learned to forge blades, used her warrior skills as a member of the Balderon Auxiliary Guard, demonstrated in competition that Emoria raises the greatest warriors in the world, and rescued her life companion from a city occupied by the Kuntians." She turned to Heko and tied the braid to her belt. "Let it be recorded that Hekolatis Ketlas is of legal age."

The crowded chanted "Heko!"

"Now it's time for Heko to lead her army to Balderon."

As the crowd shouted and chanted, Hyek walked down the platform steps followed by Heko and Niko and Zandar. They went around the back of the platform.

Hyek embraced Heko and then held her at arm's length. "Do Emoria proud and bring back a victory."

Heko took Zandar's hand and pulled her to her side. "I'll bring back a victory and Zandar's family for our ceremonial joining."

"I look forward to that," Niko said.

"Now go," Hyek said, "your army awaits you."

Heko embraced Niko, and a surprised Zandar received a hug from Hyek and Niko.

Heko turned to Zandar. "Let's go rid your city of Kuntian scum."


"I'VE IMAGINED A lot of things I'd do in my life, but this wasn't one of them." Zandar huddled between Heko and Taine in a line of Emorans in the dark against a low hollow that cut into a hill just fifteen paces from the north wall of Balderon.

"You can't say Emorans don't know how to make life interesting," Nohi said.

"The last week has been nothing but interesting," Zandar said.

The scout perched at the top of the bluff slide partway down. "The watch has been taken care of."

Heko turned to Nohi. "I predict a number of braids for the Balderon Emorans."

Nohi grinned with pride.

"Just follow me and do what I do," Heko said to Zandar. "And keep to the shadows."

Zandar took a calming breath and nodded.

"You didn't have to come along," Heko said.

"I wouldn't miss a chance to see a battle strategy in action for anything," Zandar said. "I'm ready."

Heko squeezed her hand. "Let's go."

She led a group of twenty-five warriors and scouts up a small path and over the hill. She glanced back to make sure the rest of the army that would infiltrate the city that night moved into place to follow them one group at a time.

They pattered across the short expanse of tall meadow grass and streamed into the old waste tunnel.

Lise greeted them with a welcoming grin. "Nice of you to come visit. And look, you brought friends."

"We heard that you have unwanted guests," Heko said.

"Bothersome pests," Lise said.

Heko laughed as they followed Lise's torch through the tunnel into a large damp cellar.

"All right." Heko looked at the eager faces of the women she grew up with, and who trusted her with their lives. "Remember to stay in the shadows, attack swiftly and quietly, tie and gag the Kuntians and take them to the shops and residences with this," she turned to Lise who held up a small wooden plaque with an apple carved on it, "in the window. The shopkeepers have prepared a place for the prisoners."

"An apple?" a scout asked.

"Would you be suspicious of an apple?" Heko asked. "You're going to see men. I hear the Kuntians even have some male warriors. Don't let the shock of seeing males cause you to lose focus." She completely understood the wide-eyed uncertainty that flickered in the warriors' faces. "Laur's blessing on you, and do Emoria proud."

As the warriors and scouts ghosted into the night, another group streamed in. Two sandmarks later the last Emoran left the cellar.

"Thank you, Lise," Heko said. "Good job. Now go back to the safe house and wait."

Lise looked like she wanted to argue but then nodded and trotted out of the cellar.

"Now all we have to do is get to the bakery across from the garrison," Heko said.

"No problem," Nohi said. "We practiced our scouting and tracking skills sneaking around the city at night."

"If I had only known Emorans were running around the streets at night," Zandar said.

"You would have never seen us, even if you went looking for us," Nohi said.

They stepped into the night and followed Nohi into an alley. They came to the street, and stopped and listened.

Heko put her finger to her lips and then pointed to the wall. A pair of Kuntians walked by a heartbeat later. Heko and Nohi jumped behind them and knocked them out with their dagger hilts. They caught them as they collapsed and dragged them into the alley.

"I'll go find a shop with an apple." Taine slipped into the street.

Heko turned to Zandar and was surprised to see her wide-eyed look. "What's wrong?"

"I, uh, that was incredible," Zandar said.

Heko and Nohi exchanged puzzled looks and shrugged. Taine slipped back into the alley.

"There's a shop two doors down," she said.

Heko and Nohi hefted the Kuntians onto their shoulders, and the group hurried to the shop.

"I've prepared a place back here." The shopkeeper stood from a stool in the back of the shop.

"Thank you for agreeing to do this," Heko said.

"Anything to get rid of these invaders," the shopkeeper said as they entered a small chamber.

Taine quickly bound and gagged the prisoners.

"If all goes well, horse troops will be picking them up before midday tomorrow," Heko said.

The shopkeeper put a hand on Heko's arm and looked up into her face. "You're the Emoran who beat Kiki. The rumor going around the last few days is you're a princess and you'd bring an army of Emorans to save Balderon and here you are. Thank you."

Heko could only stare at her in astonishment.

"My mother," Zandar said. "I guess there hasn't been much to do around here but get together and gossip."

"That's right," the shopkeeper said. "She told us about your rescue from Artocia and your wartime joining. We would have lost all hope if not for Ponadin's news that Emoria was going to save us."

"We'll do our best," Heko said.

"If you can lead an army like you can fight, then I have no doubt I'll be celebrating in the streets by this time tomorrow." The shopkeeper leaned over to Zandar and put her hand on her arm. "And congratulations for being joined to such a nice young woman."

Taine and Nohi stifled a laugh as Heko felt her cheeks grow warm.

# Chapter 22

"WE'RE NOT QUITE dancing jigs in the streets but close enough." Taine peeked over the roof at the Balderon military garrison. She turned to Heko. "You know, this is such a brilliant idea, I can't get over it."

"It makes this little military historian's heart go pitter patter," Zandar said. "And I get to be the one who chronicles it."

They focused their attention on several Kuntian soldiers emerging from the garrison. The soldiers looked both puzzled and agitated.

Nohi grinned. "I think they've noticed their patrols and watches haven't returned."

"Hmm. Now what would you do in their place?" Heko rubbed her chin.

"They certainly wouldn't want to exhibit any kind of panic in front of the Balderon people," Nohi said.

They watched as the Kuntians went back into the garrison.

"They'll send out the regular patrols and watches," Heko said. "Plus a few more soldiers to snoop around."

They didn't have long to wait before patrols in pairs strode through the gates. Several other soldiers, looking more casual, followed them into the streets.

Taine grinned. "The more the merrier."

"Spread the word we invade in one sandmark," Heko said.

Taine gave her a quick nod, trotted across the roof, and disappeared over the edge.

Heko cocked her head at Nohi. "It's rare for a warrior to earn her braid through battle anymore."

"That used to be the only way to earn a braid," Nohi said. "Back when we always seemed to be at war or involved in someone else's war."

"It's a much nobler way," Heko said. "Maybe we should start lending a hand more outside of Emoria."

"I know one thing." Nohi straightened. "It's been an honor to have the opportunity to serve under you."

Heko clasped Nohi's shoulder. "I'm proud to have you as a cousin."

Almost a sandmark later, Taine climbed back up onto the roof. "All the Kuntians at large have been persuaded to relax for the rest of the day."

Heko grinned. "Good." She turned to Zandar. "Whatever you see down there, stay up here until the fighting is over."

"You just be careful," Zandar said.

"Uh, we'll meet you in the alley," Taine said as she grabbed Nohi and dragged her across the roof.

Heko pulled Zandar into her arms and kissed her. "I'll be careful."

"I'll be worried every heartbeat," Zandar said, "but I know that's the price I have to pay for loving a warrior."

"I love you, too."

Heko kissed her again and reluctantly released her. She jogged across the roof, shimmied down a water spout, and landed next to Nohi and Taine.

"Ready?"

Nohi and Taine could only grin.

They ducked into the back door of a bakery. The baker looked up from kneading dough.

"Thank you for letting us use your shop," Heko said.

"If you can get rid of those Kuntians, I'll celebrate with free bread for all of you," the baker said.

"Just make enough bread for the celebration tonight," Heko said.

They went to the front of the shop, where the baker's daughter arranged loaves of bread into baskets. Invaders or not, people still came by to buy bread.

Heko ghosted to the front door and made sure the scout in the doorway of the green grocer next to the garrison building saw her. She flicked her fingers in a signal, and the scout disappeared inside the building. She then stepped away from the door.

A quarter sandmark later, they heard shouts from the garrison.

"They're discovering their unconscious comrades," Taine said.

The baker's daughter stared wide-eyed at them. "What?" she stammered.

"Our army is in there sneaking up on Kuntians and knocking them out," Heko said. "Like we've done to all the patrols and watches and any other soldier who has set foot outside the garrison."

"You're doing that for us?" the girl asked. "But you're Emorans."

"We're also a part of the Southern Territories," Heko said. "It's the least we can do for our neighbors."

The girl stared at Heko like she was a living deity.

Heko turned back to the window. The shouts and clash of steel against steel was getting louder.

"Let's cast the net." Heko turned to Nohi and Taine. They were going into battle. A moment they had all dreamed about for as long as they could remember.

Heko nodded. They pulled their masks on and stepped into the wide street. Within heartbeats, a masked Pyam and Ques came out of the buildings and signaled their regiments to form a wide semicircle in the street in front of the garrison.

The noise over the wall grew louder and closer until the gates burst open and Kuntians swarmed into the street and stopped. They gaped at the circle of Emoran warriors and then looked back at the garrison to see that way cut off by the Emorans who were routing them out.

"Attack," the Kuntian commander yelled.

Heko grinned and unsheathed her sword. Kuntians weren't known for giving up in a fight. She grinned even harder at the clatter of horses' hooves echoing through the quiet city. Most of the prisoners would be rounded up and delivered to the Southern Territories army before this skirmish would even be over.

She parried a sword, punched her adversary in the stomach, and clobbered her with her hilt. Emorans preferred to disable than kill the enemy. What was the point of dishonoring a soldier with defeat if they weren't allowed to live with that dishonor?

She whipped through one assailant after another, every bit of her being alive and vibrant. This was what she was born to do, this was what she loved to do . . . She collapsed under a blade swiping at her. For a few frightening heartbeats she tried to suck in air that wasn't there, and gasped and coughed when it finally came. She was barely aware of the blades crashing above her. She looked up and saw Nohi and Taine protecting her.

"Stay down," Taine hissed as Heko tried to stand.

"I'm fine," Heko said. "I've got to show everyone I'm fine."

"Which you're not." Taine and Nohi shielded Heko, as she stood and got her bearings.

Heko cleared her lungs with another cough and caught a blade coming at her. Taine and Nohi moved away from her, but not too far.

By that time no more Kuntians were being encouraged out of the garrison and the ones that were left looked like they were rethinking why they were fighting. The commander finally impaled a white rag in her sword and held it up.

"Cease attack!" she yelled and looked down in humiliation.

"Cease attack!" Heko yelled, and Jygar, emerging from the garrison, quickly set the warriors to round up the prisoners both conscious and unconscious.

Nohi and Taine looked around at the wounded and exhausted warriors—all with jubilant grins as they sheathed their swords.

"We did it," Taine said.

Heko sheathed her sword. "Yeah. We did."

Several Emorans were giving her questioning sidelong looks bordering on uncertainty and concern. They were just going to have to get used to the idea of an invalid princess until she fully recovered.

She turned at rapid footsteps behind her. Zandar stopped a pace away, and Heko smiled, stepped forward, and pulled Zandar into her arms. "It's all right after a battle."

"I saw your coughing fit." Zandar pulled back and gazed into Heko's eyes. "I'm not interested in witnessing something like that again. We're going to get you better before you do anything that hints of being daring or dangerous."

Heko grinned. "Is that an order?" Her heart melted at Zandar's sweet affectionate smile.

"That's an order, warrior," Zandar said.

"We're mad at you, princess."

They turned in the direction of Sarie's voice. She and Radle were emerging from the garrison with the other Balderon guards.

"You were supposed to let us go before the fighting started," Sarie said. "Now we've missed all the fun."

"The Kuntians aren't beaten yet," Heko said. "My army is headed south to help out down there."

"We'll be guarding the city," Radle said. "But that won't stop us from being envious of you."

Heko shook her head. "Not me. Just my army. I'm still recovering. And besides, I want to spend time with my life companion."

"Life companion?" Sarie turned to Zandar. "You're joined?"

"Yes," Zandar said. "When we were in Emoria."

Radle grinned. "Then we'll forgive you for forgetting to release us first. You're obviously preoccupied right now."

"A nice kind of preoccupation," Heko said.

They looked up at the sound of horses' hooves. The horse troops were converging around them.

"They've brought us our mounts," Heko said. "It's time to let the people of Balderon know their city has been liberated."

Zandar's grin was so joyous and radiant that Heko could only grin in return.

"We have banners for Balderon and Emoria." A horse warrior dropped two bundles onto the ground.

"Good." Heko opened the bundles with Zandar's help. She looked around and spotted Ques. "Ques. We need to let the people know they're not occupied anymore. Have anyone who isn't on prisoner duty find their horse and ride in groups throughout the city bearing these banners."

"Excellent idea." Ques trotted away, shouting orders.

Heko picked up a Balderon banner and handed it to Zandar and picked up an Emoran banner for herself. She mounted her horse, unsheathed her sword, and hooked a leather loop at the top of the banner over the end of the blade. The surrounding soldiers cheered and shouted, "Emoria!"

Zandar grinned and mounted her own horse. She carefully unsheathed her sword and looped the Balderon banner onto it. The soldiers cheered even louder and shouted, "Balderon!"

Taine and Nohi laughed and climbed on their horses.

Curious people peeked out their windows and doorways as the victory shouts started. They slowly gathered in the street. Some went to see if they could help with the wounded and others came out with food and drink.

Heko looked around as the groups of warriors on horseback formed around banners and guided her horse down the street.

"Ride next to me," she said to Zandar. "Turn the blade flat and brace it against the pommel."

Zandar gave her a grateful look and followed her instructions.

As the groups separated and clopped through every street they passed, the word spread fast through the alleys and by the time Heko and Zandar got to the residential merchant estates, the streets were filled with cheering jubilant people.

"Look, Mother. It's Zandar and Heko."

Heko and Zandar looked in the direction of the voice and saw little Zeck pulling on a bemused Ponadin's hand. They nudged their horses toward them.

Zandar handed her sword to Taine, gave Heko her reins, and almost fell off the horse in her excitement. She pulled her mother and brother into a hug.

Heko handed her sword to Nohi and dismounted and watched the family reunion. Happy she could make it happen in such a joyous way.

"This is like a miracle," Ponadin exclaimed.

Zandar turned to Heko. "We owe all of this to Heko."

"You didn't have to do all this to impress me," Ponadin said. Taine and Nohi stifled a laugh. "Welcome to the family." She pulled a bemused Heko into a hug.

"Thank you," Heko stammered. "I'm pleased to be a part of your family."

Ponadin turned back to Zandar. "And look at you. You look just like all these Emorans roaming about."

Zandar grinned. "The operative word is 'look.' I don't even have enough strength to hold up a sword for very long."

"Can I ride the horse?" Zeck asked.

Heko smiled down at him. "You want to be the standard bearer for Emoria?"

Taine laughed. "We won't begin to think about how many Emoran bylaws that would break."

"He's family," Heko said. "Laur won't mind."

"Heko has to finish being a hero, and I want to be with her every bit of the way," Zandar said. "We'll be back as soon as the celebrations get into full swing."

"I'm looking forward to hearing about your adventures," Ponadin said. "I want Nohi and Taine to come back, too, since they helped rescue you from Artocia."

"We'd be honored," Taine said.

Zandar embraced her mother again. "I'm so happy to see you again. I was so worried."

"I'm just glad we're all safe and sound," Ponadin said.

Heko helped Zeck to sit in front of her on the horse. She then took her sword from Nohi and gave the banner to Zeck before sheathing the blade. Zandar grinned as Taine gave her back her sword and banner.

"Look, Mother. I'm a standard bearer," Zeck cried as he waved the banner.

Taine shook her head. "Thank Laur she has a sense of humor."


BALDERON VALLEY OVERFLOWED with citizens. They had been up all night celebrating their liberation and their excitement was tempered with a good kind of exhaustion, but no one wanted to miss this important event.

City officials stood on a platform used during the festival and waited for the crowd to settle down.

Mayor Delra stepped forward and signaled for everyone's attention. She lifted a shoutbox to her lips. "The Balderon guards are going to push you back and to the sides to allow for our guests."

The audience laughed and let the guards create a space in front of the platform.

"My fellow citizens," Delra said. "We are here because we had accepted a guest to live in our city and become a part of our community and she has repaid our hospitality by bringing back an army of the greatest warriors in the world, no less, to rid our city of invaders."

The citizens of Balderon filled the valley with shouts and applause.

"We knew that Heko was an excellent warrior and guard. We knew she was polite and respectful. The one thing she neglected to mention was that she was a princess of Emoria."

The citizens laughed and applauded even louder.

"Balderon is fortunate that Hekolatis, princess of Emoria is joined with Zandar Reevler of the House of Ponadin, because this means we haven't seen the last of Heko."

The crowd chanted "Heko!" and then erupted in a deafening roar when the archers of Emoria ran out from behind a nearby low hill and fell into place before the platform. The scouts came from all directions, whooping and swinging their swords. The warriors trotted from behind the hill in three lines and ran around the other troops and then fell into place in front of them.

Following a silent command, the three forces unsheathed their swords and whipped them into a salute in precise unison. Jygar,

Pyam, and Ques rode to the front of the army and faced them. The army whipped their swords in an intricate formation and sheathed them in unison.

"Prepare to receive your princess and her consort," Jygar barked.

The army straightened and snapped their legs together. They pulled out their belt daggers and twirled them back into their sheaths. They unsheathed their swords and pointed them in the air and shouted, "Hekolatis!" and then pressed the blades to their foreheads.

Heko and Zandar trotted their horses to the front of the army and the citizens of Balderon cheered and applauded in excited abandonment. They faced the army, and Heko unsheathed her sword and returned her army's salute. She then slipped her sword back into its scabbard.

"At ease," Jygar shouted.

The army sheathed their swords and clasped their hands behind their backs.

Heko smiled at Zandar, who looked a bit dazed, and dismounted. She handed her reins to Ques and then held Zandar's horse as she dismounted.

"You'll get used to it," Heko said as they walked up the steps of the platform.

"I'll never get used to something like this," Zandar breathed.

Delra stepped up to them. "This is such an honor for our city."

"We wouldn't be good neighbors if we didn't help," Heko said.

Delra smiled as they faced the crowd.

Heko glanced at Zandar. "Relax. Make your mother proud."

Zandar sucked in a calming breath and nodded at Heko. Her smile, as always, turned Heko's insides to mush.

"Citizens of Balderon," Delra said in the shoutbox. "It is my pleasure to present Hekolatis Ketlas of Emoria with the sash of honor." She tucked a dark green sash with three golden stripes across it into Heko's shoulder plate and draped it over her upper arm. "It is also my pleasure to make Heko a citizen of Balderon."

The crowd cheered as Heko stared dumbfounded at the papers Delra put into her hands.

"It's customary for you to say something." Delra held the shoutbox to her.

Heko took the apparatus and studied it, trying to figure out how it worked while Delra silenced the crowd.

Heko held the box to her mouth. "Thank you for the honor of citizenship. I will carry it with respect and will treasure this special bond with my life companion." She smiled at Zandar, and the crowd applauded. "In return I want to make this pledge to you from Emoria. If Balderon is ever threatened by an invading army, Emoria will send an army to aid Balderon in fighting off this enemy."

The crowd shouted and applauded with such frenzy it was no use to try to quieted them down again.

"Thank you for allowing outsiders to feel welcome in your city," Heko said to Delra. "I owe the best thing that ever came into my life to Balderon and I'll never forget it." She turned to Zandar. "And as a citizen of Balderon, I can do something in public I'd never be able to do in Emoria." She wrapped Zandar into a hug and they stood arm in arm watching the citizens of Balderon pull the Emorans into their midst and offer them drinks from ale sacks and jugs.

"They can celebrate one more day," Heko said. "And then they can do Emoria proud and run those Kuntians down south back to where they belong."

# Epilogue

"OH, YOU'RE NOT going to like this." Zandar stared at the sheets of paper in her hand.

Heko looked up from the book she was taking notes from across the table. "What?"

"Mother says the people of Balderon are building a fountain in the middle of the square in front of the safe house, and they're going to put a statue of you in the middle of it."

"What?" Heko put down her pen.

"It seems that little speech you gave at the ceremony inspired them," Zandar said.

"Speech?" Heko frowned. "I don't remember giving a speech."

"You said Emoria would send an army if Balderon was ever invaded again," Zandar said.

"That wasn't a speech, that was a promise," Heko said.

Zandar sat back and gave Heko an amused look. "You can't be worried people will start staring at you."

Heko sighed. "It's just . . . I mean, I was just doing what I was raised to do. Being a warrior, a commander."

"And warriors and commanders sometimes become heroes," Zandar said.

"I'm not a—" Heko stopped, seeing Zandar's affectionate teasing in her eyes.

"It's not like we'll be spending a lot of time in Balderon," Zandar said. "We'll be splitting term breaks between Emoria and Balderon. And it'll take you four years to finish your studies here. Then you'll be my hero for being the first Emoran to have a university degree."

Heko grinned. "Day by day, I'm growing stronger both in body and in mind."

"So am I." Zandar glanced at the staff in the corner of the room. "You'll be the first Emoran to be a university scholar and I'll be the first university scholar with a warrior braid."

"Fair enough trade," Heko said. "Then we'll both be ready to rule Emoria together."

"Together?"

"Always."

T.J. Mindancer is as fictional as the Emoria Tales. She has a passing resemblance to C.A. Casey. Mindancer only pens works that take place in the Emoria Universe.

www.ingramcontent.com/pod-product-compliance
Lightning Source LLC
Chambersburg PA
CBHW031344170626
46807CB00002B/825